DRAGON MATE

THE HIDDEN KING TRILOGY

JEN L. GREY

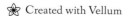 Created with Vellum

CHAPTER ONE

My phone buzzed beside me on my end table. I hadn't slept all night, nervous about this moment. Clutching my phone, I turned the alarm off and waited for any noise to indicate that someone else was up.

It was four in the morning and a safe time for Mom and Aunt Sarah to be asleep. But so much terror coursed through me that I was afraid to even breathe as I listened for anything out of the ordinary.

Pure silence greeted me.

I threw my black sheets off and stood, glancing around my dingy bedroom. The walls were off-white, and the room was only large enough for a metal, full-sized bed and an end table. The closet, positioned right across from the bed, was four feet wide at most. But it didn't matter. It wasn't like I had much stuff anyway.

My aunt had ensured I had the bare minimum, and my codependent mom never noticed. This was a four-bedroom house, and the third bedroom was twice the size of mine.

I squatted and reached under the bed. I pulled out my small duffle bag, which I'd packed last night. It sucked, but this was all I was taking to college with me. I'd buy more clothes and school supplies once I got to Kortright University, but it wasn't like I'd have more to carry if I weren't sneaking out.

After all, I couldn't stand living with my aunt for one more day. The constant insults she threw around and the way she'd smack me or worse when Mom wasn't looking had gotten out of hand. The older I got, the worse her abuse became.

I shouldered the strap of my bag as dread pooled in my stomach. What if Aunt Sarah caught me? She would do whatever was required to make me stay. She enjoyed having a punching bag.

The house remained quiet, so I headed to the door, but then I realized I'd forgotten my cell phone. I snatched it from the table and went into my settings to disable the GPS tracker.

My heart raced as I reached for the doorknob. The door tended to squeak when I opened it, so I prayed the WD-40 worked; I had put some on last night before bed. My aunt's bedroom was right beside mine so she could keep tabs on me. Mom stayed in the master bedroom downstairs, so she wouldn't hear Sarah's and my violent fights.

As I slowly opened the door, my body sagged with relief, until the door groaned right at the end. Dammit, I'd almost opened it the entire way.

Something bumped in Sarah's room. "Jadie?"

I hated that nickname, and she knew it. That was why she insisted on calling me that. Hell, I wasn't really a fan of Jade, either. My eyes and hair were dark, and my skin tone was olive. Why had my parents named me that?

My head grew dizzy from me holding my breath. It

wasn't like she could hear me breathe, but I didn't want to chance it. Maybe she'd go back to sleep.

Of course, that was when something hit the ground. It had to be her feet.

"Damn, girl," she muttered as her footsteps headed to the door. "If you're trying to sneak out after all I've done for you, I'll beat you to a bloody pulp," she said loudly.

There was no getting out of this gracefully. I inhaled sharply and took off down the hall. I needed to get to the stairs before she beat me there and woke up Mom to play the role of needy mother. I always caved.

I reached the stairs right as her door opened.

"Get your ass back here!" she yelled, stepping into the hallway. Her long caramel hair was disheveled, and her cold, ice-blue eyes stared at me with disgust. "Where do you think you're going?"

She expected me to obey, but not today. I had to take this chance ... for me. I barreled down the stairs and heard her running after me. When I hit the bottom of the stair-case, Sarah rounded the corner and bounded down behind me.

Dammit. She was in almost as good of shape as I was, but I had youth on my side. By the time I unlocked the front door, Sarah was halfway down the stairs. I yanked the door open and raced out to the front yard.

The middle-income neighborhood was quiet and dark, without a light on in any house. Everyone was still sleeping like Sarah should have been.

I ran left, hoping my crappy, old Toyota Corolla was still parked in the dead end. I'd bought the car only ten hours ago for this escape. It was the only thing I could afford without blowing all of my savings.

Sarah slammed the front door shut as she ran out into the yard. "Stop running this instant."

No, that was definitely not happening.

I ignored the command and channeled all of my energy into getting away. Adrenaline pumped through me, but I could hear her gaining on me. The duffle bag was making it so damn hard to run.

Right as I reached the edge of our half-acre front yard, Sarah slammed into my back. I fell to my knees hard, and she kicked me in the side.

"Do you know what happens to people who disobey me?" Sarah hissed and kicked me again.

Pain throbbed deep in my side, but I refused to let her know how much it hurt. I understood physical pain and welcomed it on occasion, just not when I had so much at stake.

She pulled her leg back to kick me again, and my instincts took over. I caught her foot and lifted, throwing her off balance. She landed on her back.

The one good thing Mom had done for me since Dad had died was put me in martial arts and self-defense classes to make sure I could protect myself in ways she never could. It was part of the reason she was so broken now; she felt responsible for Dad's death.

"How dare you!" Sarah groaned and rolled onto her side.

A dog barked in the distance, and a light turned on in the neighbor's house directly across from us.

We were going to wake up the whole neighborhood, which was partly her goal. If she could make the neighbors come out, she could manipulate them into getting me back inside. She'd lied about things I'd done before.

I climbed to my feet and adjusted the shoulder strap as I

prepared to take off again toward the car. I had to lose her before she could see my car and get my license plate number. She'd have the police searching for me within minutes. I had to figure something out. Each passing moment jeopardized my escape.

My aunt grabbed my foot, and I again found myself falling forward onto the grass. Then it hit me.

I had no choice.

I had to fight her.

She crawled over to me and punched me in the ear. A loud ringing pierced my brain.

Tossing the bag a few feet away, I ignored the sound and turned toward her. I punched her in the nose.

The bones crunched, and blood ran from both nostrils.

I grimaced internally, knowing Mom would be mortified and ashamed when she heard about this. But I needed to do this even if it was selfish.

"You." Her eyes narrowed into slits, and she spat on the ground. "That won't slow me."

I was sure it wouldn't. Crazy held no limits.

Getting into a fighter stance, I made it clear I wouldn't back down. "Good. This is long overdue." I was bluffing. I didn't want to hurt her even though she took every opportunity to cut me down. I needed to knock her out or force her to retreat into the house. The latter wasn't an option for her, though.

"Yes, it is." She used the back of her pajama shirt to wipe the blood from her mouth. "I've always held back, but not now."

That was a lie. One day, she'd punched me so hard she'd broken her hand. But I'd try the bare minimum to convince her to back off.

"I'm giving you one last chance." Sarah breathed

raggedly. "Get back in the house now, or I will make your face unrecognizable."

"No," I said slowly and with force. That wouldn't happen.

She tried to knee me between the legs, but I'd anticipated the cheap shot. I took a few steps back and kicked her in the stomach. She flew back a few feet and landed on her ass.

Not giving her a chance to stand, I rushed behind her and wrapped my arm around her neck. I tightened my arm around her, cutting off her oxygen.

As I waited for her to pass out, I kept my eyes on the neighbor's front door. She hadn't come out yet. Granted, she could be watching from the window. I had to get out of here.

Sarah dug her nails into my arm. Blood pooled under her fingertips as she desperately tried to get me off her, but I pushed through the pain.

Just as the pain became unbearable, her hold on my arm slackened. The lack of air was finally making a difference. Within the next few seconds, she'd be out cold.

The front door of the house across the street opened, and the older woman peeked out. When her eyes landed on us, her mouth dropped. She gasped, "Oh, dear God," and shut the door.

She'd be calling the cops.

Sarah's head rolled to the side, and I released my hold, gently putting her on the ground. If the neighbor hadn't seen us, I would've put her inside the house, but I had to cut my losses.

I ran over, grabbed my bag, and ran for my life.

My HANDS SHOOK as I drove toward Kortright University. An hour ago, Mom called over and over to the point where I turned my cell phone off and chucked it before Sarah had the cell phone company track me. I managed to grab a prepay one at Wal-Mart a few miles back and was finally able to use the GPS to find the University without worrying about being located.

It was ridiculous. I kept glancing in my cracked rearview mirror, expecting to find a cop car chasing me. No one knew this was my car, and I'd parked far enough away that the neighbors hadn't seen me drive away. For all they knew, I was on foot, which would bode well for me.

The phone rang, startling me. How the hell had Mom gotten this number? That should have been impossible.

I glanced at the caller ID, and my shoulders sagged. It was a number I'd never seen before, proving I was way too anxious. I had to calm down before I did something stupid like wreck my car. The vehicle couldn't survive a hard bump, let alone a fender bender.

Kortright University's all-brick sign became visible, and butterflies took flight in my stomach.

It was real. I had made it to Hidden Ridge, Tennessee. For a second back there, all had seemed lost, but here I was, further validating that this was destiny.

As I turned onto the street that led to the school, I suddenly felt self-conscious. I passed by brand-new Hondas, SUVs, and a few BMWs.

I stuck out like a sore thumb, which was never a good thing. Blending in had always been my motto.

None of that mattered. It was only a stupid car I would rarely drive. I drove past the large-ass stadium as football players ran around its perimeter, wearing gold shirts and black shorts—the university's signature colors.

This school had been around for over a hundred years and had quite the reputation—another reason I'd been surprised to get a full ride mid-school year.

I found myself in a large parking lot close to two huge buildings. From all the pictures I'd seen, those were the dorms.

My car squealed as I pulled into the closest parking spot. A couple of guys a few cars down chuckled at me.

Whatever. I wasn't trying to impress them.

With as much dignity as I could muster, I shouldered my strap and climbed out of the car. I tried not to visibly cringe as the door groaned shut.

The guys hollered, but I held my head high and walked past them, pretending they didn't exist. I didn't need anyone anyway. Getting close to people only got you hurt or in trouble.

I marched to the sidewalk, on a mission to find my room and settle in. I needed time to decompress after the hellacious start to my day.

But when I turned the corner to walk past the boys' dorm, I stopped in my tracks, unable to process what I saw as drool pooled at the corner of my mouth.

CHAPTER TWO

I blinked. I had to be imagining this. The sexiest guy I'd ever seen was walking towards the front door of the boys' dorm.

He was easily seven feet tall, a good thirteen inches taller than me, and built like a freaking Ford truck. He wore a simple, loose, royal blue t-shirt, but it molded to his muscular chest and arms. His blue jeans also hugged his body in all of the ways they should on a man, but he might as well have been wearing sweatpants because his manhood was outlined. His longish blond hair was styled upward with matching scruff on his chin.

I'd never felt drawn to any guy before, so it caught me by complete surprise.

My gawking must have caught his attention because his golden eyes turned to me, and his pupils turned to slits.

Slits. That was freaking impossible.

I tore my gaze from him, freaked out by the experience. I was both turned on and petrified.

Forcing my feet to move, I pretended that nothing had

happened. I kept my eyes forward and focused on putting one foot in front of the other.

Something inside me knew he was watching me. Without permission, my head turned back toward him, and I almost cried in relief when his pupils were normal. Sleep deprivation had hit me hard, causing me to imagine things.

He stepped toward me, and everything inside yelled at me to flee. I jerked my head forward and picked up my pace. Part of me wanted to go to him, which made the rest of me more desperate to get away. A guy could destroy you. That was what had happened to Mom. I never wanted to end up like her.

"Hey, wait up," the guy called out. His accent was strange and alluring. I'd never heard one like it before.

Without acknowledging him, I continued on like I either hadn't heard him or thought he was talking to someone else. In all fairness, he could have been. There was nothing special about me.

I forced him out of my mind and focused on the weather. Knoxville was a good twenty degrees warmer than Indianapolis. Of course, my rushing around probably kept me warm too. My blood was definitely flowing.

I entered the dorm and stopped at the front desk. A girl with light brown hair pulled into a ponytail looked up from her cell phone. Her chestnut brown eyes locked on me, and she arched an eyebrow. "How can I help you?"

"Oh, um." I pointed at my duffle bag like that should make it obvious. "I'm new here. I need to find which dorm room I'm assigned to."

"Yeah, okay." She tapped a clipboard a few times. "Are you Jade Storm?"

"That's me." I tried to make my voice sound light, but it fell flat ... and sarcastic. This was why I avoided people.

"Alrighty then." Huffing, she reached into the drawer and pulled out an envelope with 501 written on it. "Here you go."

"Thanks." In an attempt to avoid making the encounter even more awkward, I turned and scanned the lobby.

For an older school, this surprised me. Single light bulbs hung from the ceiling every few feet, and the walls were a medium gray. A group of couches created a huge square in the center of the wide-open space, each one a different primary color that offset the walls.

Straight back sat a large elevator with a door on each far side of the wall that had to be the stairwells. I already felt underdressed in my holey jeans, which hadn't been designed that way, and the thin sweater hanging off my frame. The few girls I'd passed were dressed in trendy outfits such as skinny jeans, boots, and cute fitted sweaters.

I rushed past the couches, ignoring the strange looks thrown my way. I hit the button on the elevator and prayed the double doors would open and swallow me whole. I needed time alone, which was crazy, seeing as I'd driven for over five hours in the car by myself.

Whispers filled the air, choking me. As the weird loner, no one wanted to associate with, I'd been made fun of throughout high school. Sure, guys would hit on me, but they always only wanted one thing. It was like a challenge to them since I never paid any of them any attention.

The doors slid open to reveal four of the most beautiful girls I'd ever seen. The most striking one was in the center. Her shoulder-length, rose-gold hair and piercing blue eyes would have stopped any guy in his tracks. She was a tad shorter than the striking redhead, who had her head thrown back in laughter, but not by much.

"Oh my God, Roxy." The brown-haired girl at the end

cringed, narrowing her light brown eyes, which had an auburn tint to them. "We don't want to hear about your sexcapades with Axel."

"Speak for yourself." The girl with black hair and even darker eyes laughed. Her eyes had a red hue that made them unique and gorgeous. She wore a long-sleeved, flowy black shirt with dark jeans. "I'm not getting any, so I have to live vicariously through someone. Sadie doesn't kiss and tell."

"I don't want you thinking of Donovan that way." Her blue eyes glowed faintly. "He's all mine."

The air around them was comforting, unlike most girl cliques I'd seen. They didn't have jealousy or animosity floating off them. For the first time ever, I was jealous.

"Hey," the girl I assumed was Sadie said gently as her eyes locked on mine, "are you okay?"

What? Reality swooped back in on me when I realized I was blocking them from exiting the elevator. Once again, I was gawking. "Yeah, sorry." I moved aside and waved them on, waiting for their laughter.

But none of them laughed.

Instead, the girl with the lighter brown hair smiled. "It's no problem."

The four of them walked by me more gracefully than I'd ever seen anyone move. I'd have bet they had their pick of any guy they set their sights on.

I jumped into the elevator as the girls on the couches snickered again. Now *they* were cold-hearted bitches who were only out for themselves.

On the fifth floor, the number of girls chattering in the hallways almost overwhelmed me. After scanning the area, I turned right and headed to the very end of the hall. My room was the last one on the right.

The fact that I wouldn't have to deal with neighbors on both sides excited me way too much. I unlocked the door and walked in.

The room was four times the size of my bedroom at my aunt's. Twin beds sat across from each other against the light gray walls. A small window in front of the unclaimed bed overlooked the boys' dorm. A desk occupied the space at the foot of the bed, no wider than the bed itself, leaving enough space for me to walk around it to look out the window. The half of the dorm room that would be considered mine gave me more than enough space to feel comfortable.

I'd learned how to live minimally at Sarah's. When Mom and I had moved in after Dad died, Aunt Sarah had sworn up and down that she needed the third bedroom that had been twice the size of the room I wound up occupying for storage. The kicker was that the room wasn't close to a quarter full. I'd been eight years old and had just lost my father, but it had rubbed me wrong even then. Yet, this had been just a tiny taste of what the next ten years had been like for me. Still, at least it prepared me for dorm living.

Brushing off the memory, I entered the room, and a short, thin girl who wore glasses with thick, dark plastic frames faced me. Her stringy caramel hair hung down her face and across her sable eyes. She wore a white Star Wars shirt and plaid pants.

Her outfit was interesting, which was saying a lot coming from me.

When my eyes met hers, she jerked forward and stiffened. She was breathing so hard I could hear her from five feet away.

"Uh ... hi." I wasn't sure what to do, but if we were going to be roommates, I couldn't be a complete ass, could I?

"H-hi," she stuttered and moved her focus back onto a textbook on her desk. "I was hoping I'd have the room to myself again, especially since it's halfway through the school year."

At least, she was as socially awkward as I was. That would either work out well for both of us or be a complete disaster. Only time would tell. "My name is Jade."

She tugged at her ear and kept her eyes cast downward. "I'm Vera."

I glanced at her side of the room and winced internally at the Star Wars sheets on her bed and the poster against her wall. Our room had a sort of style.

The fact that she'd picked the side of the room that butted up against our dorm neighbor surprised me. I'd gotten the side that I preferred. "What's wrong with the bed?" That was the only explanation why she'd choose the lesser side.

"Nothing." She cleared her throat and bent over, hiding her face from me. "It's just ..."

"What?" Before settling in, I wanted to know what I was up against. Bed bugs? Lumpy mattress?

She cringed. "I'm a—afraid of heights."

I hadn't expected that. The window was three feet above the bed and small. It would take a lot of effort to fall through it. It would have to be purposeful, not an accident. "Okay." I nodded, trying to keep my expression indifferent.

"Please don't make fun of me." Her bottom lip quivered. "I know girls like you don't understand what having irrational fears must be like."

"Girls like me?" Just when I'd thought she was timid.

"Beautiful and confident." She waved at me. "I won't bother you, I promise."

I'd never been described like that before. "Thank you, but I'm neither one of those things, and there is no reason I'd make fun of you." I understood what it was like to be cut down each and every day.

She licked her lips. "Okay."

Silence descended between us as I unpacked my bag and made my bed with the light sheets I'd brought. I hung up my clothes in the closet right behind my desk.

It was kind of sad. Within five minutes, I'd unpacked everything I'd brought. "Is the bookstore open?"

"Yes, for another hour or two." She peeked up, looking at my chin, avoiding my eyes. "If you need books, now's the time to get them."

"No shit," was on the tip of my tongue, but I bit it back. That'd been the whole reason I'd asked. "Got it." I grabbed the cash from my duffle bag and walked out of the room. I wouldn't find peace until I felt somewhat prepared for tomorrow.

I took the stairs to the first floor. That way, I wouldn't have to pass the fakers.

At the bottom, I took the side door instead of going through the lobby. A chilly breeze hit me as I stepped outside.

I'd have to buy a jacket soon. In my haste to leave Sarah's, I hadn't thought to grab one.

I wrapped my arms around myself and hurried to the building right across from the girls' dorm. According to the map, it had to be the Student Center where the bookstore and cafeteria were. My stomach grumbled at the thought of food, but I wanted to get my books first.

I hurried along the white concrete sidewalk between the two buildings. Several groups hung out at the benches, and three huge oak trees shaded the entire area. Even with the cool breeze, people were unaffected here.

The back entrance to the Student Center appeared, and I rushed over, wanting to get out of the cold. A strong gust of wind slammed the door shut behind me.

I practically jumped out of my skin.

Dammit, I was way too on edge.

To my right was the university bookstore. I glanced inside and realized that most of the books had been picked through. I'd been banking on purchasing used books. This meant I needed to find a job as soon as possible.

A few students were doing last-minute shopping like me, including—no. Tall, blond, and sexy was across the room, scanning the science section.

That was fine. I'd get that book last. I figured he should be out of here by then. I rushed to the English section on the opposite side of the store. I found the book and moved on to find the other two.

Now, I only needed my science book. I glanced over at that section and found him still standing there. What the hell? Were all of his classes science?

I considered checking out and coming back later. Then it occurred to me that I was letting a man affect my decision, breaking my most important rule: I would never give anyone that much power over me.

I straightened my shoulders and marched over to the science section. I was making way too much over this. It wasn't like the guy would notice me. He screamed "important," and he'd need someone wearing Versace or whatever the hell those designer clothes were called on the girl standing beside him.

Steadying myself, I walked down the aisle, looking for

the Chemistry 101 book. Of course, as I walked past the Biology and Physics sections, I noticed the book I was looking for was at the end, right next to him. *So, he must be taking that class too.*

My heart pounded, and I was so damn glad that no one but I could hear it. How did simply looking at someone make me turn into this pathetic girl I refused to be? Even if my nerves were raw, I'd be damned if he ever knew it.

He stood directly in front of the stack of books I needed, but I could do this. I had to prove it to myself. I cleared my throat, but he kept scanning the books. The only hint that he might have heard me was the corner of his mouth tipping upward.

"Excuse me." I cleared my throat even louder, glaring at him. My annoyance made me feel better. Maybe I was over-reacting. "I need to get that book."

"Sure," he said, his faint accent catching me off guard. "I'm sorry." He stepped out of the way, but his huge body was still partially in front of it.

Fine. It was fine. I reached past him, making sure not to touch him, and snatched the book as fast as possible. I turned and rushed away, taking the long way out so I wouldn't have to walk past him. I'd been close enough only moments ago.

No one was in line at the cash register, so I rushed to the front and threw all of my books down on the counter.

The guy behind the counter raised an eyebrow and shrugged, ringing up each book and notepad. When he read off the total, my stomach churned. I didn't have enough on me. "Oh, can I leave these here and run back to get more money?" I hadn't imagined school books would cost this much. The day had progressively gotten worse. My throat dried as tears burned my eyes. I'd have to look for a job tomorrow if not tonight.

When a huge presence appeared beside me, I wished to become invisible.

CHAPTER THREE

I didn't have to look to know it was him. His presence towered over me. What I didn't understand was why he was here.

"Is there a problem?" Dead Sexy asked, and my stomach tightened.

His voice added to his allure. Maybe I needed to invest in earplugs for when he was around. Wait ... no. That wasn't the solution. The real answer was keeping my distance.

The cashier nodded. "Yeah—"

"No," I cut him off. I refused to be humiliated more than I already was. "There's no problem. I just need to run back to the dorm and get more cash." Not eating a large dinner would teach me self-discipline, which I was obviously lacking, thanks to Golden Eyes.

Ugh, I wasn't sure which nickname was worse: Golden Eyes or Dead Sexy. Both made my heart flip-flop. Stupid, traitorous heart.

Golden Eyes placed his books down beside mine.

"Here, ring mine up too." He pulled out a credit card and set it on the counter. "I'll get both of ours."

"What?" Did he think I needed a handout? "Thanks, but no. I have enough back at the dorm."

"It's cold, and you don't have a jacket." He frowned as he glanced at my clothes. "This will keep you from getting sick."

"What are you, my mother?" I cringed; I was being rude. I didn't mean to be, but for him to buy my schoolbooks put red flags up everywhere. No one did anything nice unless they expected something in return. I blurted, "I won't sleep with you."

The cashier snorted and covered it up with a cough.

"Damn, Egan," a guy said, not three feet from us.

I snapped my head in the newcomer's direction and wished I could turn back time. I wouldn't have gotten the damn chemistry book.

The guy who'd spoken had buzzed dark hair and was only a few inches taller than me. His dark eyes filled with mirth. "You just got burned."

"Axel." The third guy, who was taller and even more handsome, chuckled beside him. He was larger than his friend but only half the size of Golden Eyes—Egan. He had longish black hair and piercing blue eyes. A tribal tattoo peeked past his short-sleeved shirt on his right arm.

Who wore short sleeves in winter? And here Egan was, concerned about my lack of a jacket. He needed to worry about his friends.

Egan ignored them and handed the cashier the credit card. "No sex is expected."

"Or blow jobs. Anything sexual is off the table." Why couldn't I shut up? It was like all logic had left me.

His friends tried not to laugh, but smirks were sliding right across their faces.

"Nothing is asked of you." Egan's face turned red as he pushed the card toward the stunned cashier. "It's really not a big deal."

Those books cost more than I earned in a week back at the Italian restaurant I had worked at. The tips hadn't been great but steady. So this was a huge deal. However, I'd already been rude enough, and honestly, I could use the help.

Taking the card, the cashier swiped it, obviously uncomfortable and wanting me to go away. I couldn't blame him. Awkward silence grew thick around Egan, his friends, the cashier, and me.

"We're heading to the cafeteria," the taller friend said. "Want us to save you a seat?"

"You know he does." Axel snorted. "The guy will probably eat most of the food anyway."

"Maybe you and Roxy aren't such a good thing," the other guy replied. "You've gotten more of a mouth on you since you two became ma—a couple."

Mae? I had no clue what he'd been about to say, but he'd obviously changed the wording because of me, piquing my curiosity.

No, Jade. Interest in people was not allowed. I had enough on my plate, without adding more complications, because that was what any relationship created.

Egan took the card back from the cashier and signed the receipt. "I'll be right there."

The two guys waved and headed off.

The cashier divided up Egan's and my books and handed us each a bag. At least, he was smart. I grabbed my bag and stayed put. After him buying my books for me, it wasn't like I could run away. So far, he'd only been nice. It wasn't his fault I found his damn sexy ass attractive.

After putting his wallet in his back pocket, he took his bag and held his right hand out to me.

That was a new one, but okay. I quickly and limply shook his hand. The less touching we did, the better. My fingers buzzed when I touched him, telling me way too much. This was the type of stuff I'd overheard girls describe right before their hearts got destroyed beyond recognition. Yet another reminder of why I needed to gain distance.

He chuckled and shook his head. "No, I was going to carry your bag for you. All those books are heavy."

"You don't think I can handle it?" This wasn't anything. I lifted weights six times as heavy every day.

"What? No." He lifted his hand. "That's not what I meant. It's just, you're a lady—"

"So I need a strong, burly man like you to help me?" He considered me helpless, and it infuriated me.

He blew out a breath. "This is all coming out wrong." He dropped his hand in defeat. "I was trying to be a gentleman."

Maybe that was the truth, but it didn't improve the situation. I tried to swallow my anger, except the best I could do was turn it into annoyance. "I can pay you back." I held out the money I had in my back pocket. "I'm only short a hundred. If you let me run back to the dorm—"

"That was the whole point." He waved the money away. "And it's fine. I don't mind doing that for you."

"Look, at least, take this." He was making me feel pathetic even if he didn't mean to. It was important that I stand on my own two feet. He was a strong man, so he wouldn't understand. "It'll make me feel better."

"It would make you feel better?" His brows furrowed. "Really?"

If I hadn't been so upset, the confusion on his face would have been comical. I wondered how many girls he'd done this for. Obviously, none of the others had complained. "Yes, that's a lot of money, and I just need to do this."

"But it's no big deal." His shoulders sagged in disappointment.

"It is to me." He looked like he was crumbling, so I applied more pressure. "I really do appreciate it." And I did. By him covering what I didn't have, I'd have enough money to eat for a few days if I budgeted. I'd have to go find a job and run to the grocery store. I'd be eating a lot of PB&Js. I held out the money, needing him to take it.

He pursed his lips and scratched the back of his neck. "Okay."

Once he'd taken the money, I turned, ready to get the hell out of there. Since he was meeting his friends at the cafeteria, I'd skip lunch and come back later to grab dinner. In the meantime, I'd raid the vending machine downstairs in the dorm. Besides, I didn't have any cash on me to get food even if I wanted to.

"Hey," he called right as I entered the hallway.

I wished he'd leave me alone. The more time I spent around him, the harder it would be to keep my distance. I wasn't sure how I knew that, but I felt it in my bones. On their own accord, my feet stopped and turned me around. "Yeah?"

"My friends and I are grabbing lunch." He placed a hand in his jeans pocket. "Why don't you join us?"

This guy couldn't be real. He actually seemed decent, which scared me. Assholes I could handle, but sincere people petrified me. "Remember, I don't have any more cash." I forced a grin. "But thanks." I couldn't remember the last time someone had invited me to hang out with them.

He took a few eager steps toward me. "I can buy your lunch."

"You just covered a hundred bucks on my books." My head screamed at me to run. "Thanks, but no. Have fun with your friends." I took off again, back to my dorm, needing to clear my head.

MY ALARM BLARED, barely waking me from a deep sleep. After the traumatic start to my day, I'd passed out hard last night, but I didn't feel any better. I'd dreamt about Mom and Dad and the day before he died. It was strange. We'd gone to the beach as a family and had the best day. I'd even made a friend, whom I'd felt like I'd known all my life even though we'd just met. At first, my parents had hung out with his parents, and they'd all gotten along until something had freaked out Mom.

I hadn't dreamed or thought of that day in so long. It hurt too much. It was the last time everything had felt perfect in my life.

Vera grumbled, "Are you going to turn that thing off?" She put her pillow over her head.

Good to know she had the dramatic air of a normal teenage girl. I'd started to think she was abnormal, which wouldn't have been a bad thing. After I'd gotten back from the bookstore, we'd kept to ourselves. Being roommates might work out for both of us.

"Yeah, sorry." I snagged the phone off the ground and

stopped the alarm. All I wanted to do was go back to sleep, but then I'd be late for my class.

I had to take this seriously since I ran away for this opportunity when fall semester hadn't panned out at the local community college. Mom and I agreed that I'd attend there for the fall semester. We'd compromised since Mom didn't want me to leave. I'd at least get an education. But when Aunt Sarah had found out about our little plan, she'd informed Mom that if I went to college instead of getting a job to help cover our expenses, we'd have to move out. Mom had broken down, and I'd done the only thing I could: I'd let the opportunity go—or I'd planned to.

But when I'd stumbled upon an online ad for Kortright University. Something had pulled at me stronger than ever before. This was the place for me, so I did what I had to do. I'd paid for a post office box and applied. I hadn't expected it to amount to much since it was a private college, but then they'd offered to cover my tuition, including room and board, and only books and other expenses were my responsibility. I'd have to work, but the brunt of the financial burden had been eliminated. I'd considered it destiny.

With every ounce of strength I had, I put my feet on the shaggy brown carpet and stood. I hadn't showered after my rumble with Sarah, so that was a necessity. I grabbed the one towel I'd brought and a change of clothes and forced myself to enter the realm of an all-girl bathroom.

It was worse than I'd expected for nine in the morning, but luckily, I got the last shower stall and was in and out within minutes.

Back in the safety of my room, I sighed with relief as I finished toweling off my hair, slipping on a pair of ripped jeans and a long-sleeved shirt. As usual, I didn't put on makeup. I had no one to impress anyway.

I grabbed the textbooks I needed for my first day, a folder, and some cash for breakfast. Since I didn't have a bag to carry my items in yet, it was a little awkward, but I'd make it work.

I'd wound up hiding out for the remainder of the night in my dorm, eating Doritos and Funyuns instead of going back to the Student Center. I hated to admit it, but I'd been too nervous that I might run into him yet again, so I'd stayed put. Those two run-ins with him had been more than enough.

The buzz of conversations hit me when I entered the Student Center. I scanned the wide-open area of booths and tables, and most of them were full. It felt like high school all over again. Everyone had their clique, and I was the outsider.

I made a beeline toward the food counter on my left. There were ten different service stations, and each one was pretty full. It surprised me that there were so many options. The pictures on the internet hadn't done them any justice.

Saliva pooled in my mouth as I considered the different options. When I spotted the fresh cinnamon rolls one of the workers put out, I practically ran right to them.

I snagged two and a cup of coffee and headed straight to the cash register. On my way, my eyes found him—Golden Eyes. Wow, when his friends had said he ate almost all of the food, they hadn't been lying.

Egan had two trays, and each one was full of every type of breakfast. It had to cost at least fifty dollars, all in one sitting. Who could afford to eat like that?

Didn't matter. It wasn't any of my business. I forced my focus back in front of me and quickly checked out before I had yet another run-in with him.

The safest spot for me was outside, despite the chill.

After class today, I'd go find a job and pick up a jacket. I marched right outside and sat at a bench in the sunshine. It wasn't quite as bad there.

Taking a bite, I enjoyed the cinnamon and vanilla frosting that hit my tongue. I hadn't had a cinnamon roll in years. Well, about ten years. That was what Dad would make me every morning on my birthday. It had been my favorite growing up. The fact I was now eating one wasn't lost on me. Maybe I could finally put a little bit of the pain behind me.

The pink-haired girl from the other day walked out of the Student Center and frowned when she saw me. "Hey, are you okay?"

I looked around, expecting to see one of her friends, but then I realized she was talking to me. "Uh ... yeah. Why?"

"You look sad." She made her way over, watching me with a tilt of her head. "And you're sitting out here alone while it's chilly by Tennessee standards. Did something happen?"

Maybe I wasn't leaving any of my pain behind after all. "Yeah, I'm fine. Just a little overwhelmed." I wanted to slap my hands over my mouth. Why had I said that to her?

"You're new here." She nodded. "Are you lost or something?"

Her question hit me hard. "Yeah, I am." But I didn't mean it in the way she thought. I meant lost in life. It was probably the most honest moment I'd had in a long time.

"Then where are you heading?" The girl smiled, somehow becoming even more breathtaking.

"American History." At least I knew that off the top of my head.

"I am too." Her sky-blue eyes lit up with enthusiasm. "Come with me." She gestured for me to follow her.

Eh ... I could eat the other cinnamon roll in class. I stood, gathered my things, and walked beside her, feeling awkward. I wasn't used to talking to people my own age.

As we strolled past a Student Center window, the back of my neck tingled, alerting me that someone was watching me. My heart raced, and the urge to flee overwhelmed me.

CHAPTER FOUR

The chill sank deep into my bones. It felt like the times Sarah would be watching me through the window, thinking I hadn't noticed her.

It was creepy, unsettling, and straight-up disturbing.

The rose-gold-haired girl stopped and turned to me. "Is something wrong?"

"Nope," I said way too quickly. Great, let's add paranoid to my list of winning personality traits. I picked up my pace and glanced over my shoulder. Something flashed behind a tree by the side of the building as if they were hiding from me.

It was probably a cat, rabbit, squirrel, or some other animal that hung around during the colder months. It wasn't like it was a person. But I couldn't shake that feeling. No wonder talking to people gave me such anxiety.

"So, I'm Sadie." She gestured to herself.

The name suited her. "A unique name for a unique girl."

Her eyebrow lifted, and a corner of her mouth turned upright. "Um ... thanks?"

"Unique as in different." Oh, God. I'd just insulted her when all she'd done was be nice to me. "I mean, you're pretty."

She chuckled. "Are you going to share your name with me?"

"Jade." I tried pointing at myself but wound up shoving the plastic food container into my chest, nearly popping it open, and coffee sloshed out and trickled down my hand.

"Do you need help?" She held out her hand to take the container. "You need to get a backpack or a bag or something."

Yeah, I did. But I'd have to wait until I found a job. Right when I was about to tell her no, that I had it, she took the container out of my hand.

"Let me get the coffee too." She snatched the coffee and picked up the pace, leaving me behind.

Adjusting the books, I hurried to catch up. "Thanks." I jostled the books to one side and wiped my hand against my jeans to remove the coffee.

"No problem," she said, eyeing me like she expected me to snatch the food and drink back.

Part of me wanted to, but I ignored the urge. Yes, I'd mainly come to college to get away from my aunt and make something of my life, but maybe I could be a little more open with people. Like, not go crazy by dating or anything but, at least, have an acquaintance I could copy notes from if I missed a class.

Even thinking about dating had my heart beating erratically, but I couldn't become a weird, reclusive cat lady, could I?

The thought wasn't all that unappealing, proving how bad I'd gotten.

Instead of continuing down my train wreck line of

thoughts, I focused on our surroundings. We headed right, passing the sidewalk that led to Kortright Stadium, and stayed on the path of the large circle, passing Wilson Hall. American History was held in Grey Hall, which sat across the grassy area from the Student Center with Webster Hall to the left and Wilson Hall directly opposite.

As we approached the standard two-story brick building, I observed the students buzzing by. Our class was on the top floor. If memory served me right, there wasn't an elevator in this building. The entryway was flat, and I held the large single door open for Sadie. It only seemed right since she was carrying my food and drink. It also helped that she knew where she was going. I followed her as she turned right to the single stairway that headed upstairs before entering the large hallway of the main floor.

People squeezed past us as we walked up the narrow stairway barely wide enough for two people to pass by comfortably.

I should've taken my stuff back from Sadie. If her clothes got ruined, I couldn't afford to buy her any new ones.

But I soon learned I didn't need to worry. Even as people shoved past her, she had the most grace I'd ever seen before. It was like she anticipated the movements before they jarred her and shifted to prevent anything from spilling on her.

I was extremely envious. Even with all the martial arts, I still tripped over my own feet.

On the top floor, Sadie entered the first classroom on the right, and I dutifully followed. There were four rows with eight seats each. The classroom was half full, and most of the front seats were already taken.

Odd.

Didn't everyone get to class early to sit at the back? That was always my motivation.

Sadie walked past the first two rows toward the back. She glanced over her shoulder. "Mind if we sit back there?"

"Nope." That was exactly what I preferred. Maybe we were meant to be friends.

Two guys in the middle almost broke their necks to watch Sadie walk by. Girls like her commanded attention even though it wasn't on purpose, unlike the popular kids back in high school, who would flip their hair and wear revealing clothing to capture guys' attention. Sadie wore jeans that weren't skin tight and a thick, black sweater that was stylish yet simple. Her hair was short compared to most girls our age, and her face was gorgeous despite wearing very little makeup.

As I walked past another row over, no one turned my way, which was fine. I didn't want the attention anyway. I plopped into the desk next to Sadie and dropped my Spanish book on the ground.

"Here you go." Sadie held out my food and coffee.

"Thanks for the help." Those were words I wasn't used to saying.

"No problem," she said as she set her purple backpack on the ground and pulled out her own items. She got situated as I finished my food.

A petite girl entered the room. Her teal eyes, which matched the shade of her hair, locked on Sadie, and a smile spread across her face, emphasizing the golden-pink hue of her skin. What was it with the girls here? This girl was gorgeous too.

"Sadie," she said, and her voice sounded like a bell. She rushed toward the back and took the other seat beside her.

"Naida." Sadie sounded thrilled to see her. "How are you? It's been a few weeks."

"Yes, I'm sorry." Naida's voice held a slight accent similar to Golden Eyes. "Just everything is crazy in Fae—"

"The family." Sadie laughed loudly then cringed. "Those damn family members."

"Right," Naida agreed, and her eyes brushed over me. "They are something."

It was obvious they didn't want me to know what they were talking about. Maybe I'd misjudged them. I kept my eyes forward, not bothering to glance at them. I recognized when people were excluding me.

***

CLASS ENDED, and I grabbed my books and stood, eager to get the hell out. I tried to be patient with all of the people in front of me, but I didn't want Sadie to feel obligated to talk to me. As long as I looked busy, she'd be off the hook. It helped that Naida had leaned over and begun whispering right when class was dismissed.

Every seat had been taken since this was a fundamental class at a coveted university. I'd bet all my classes would be packed.

Luckily, my next class was in the same building, only on the first floor. People finally moved out of my way, and when I stepped into the hallway, I breathed a little easier. I bounded down the stairs and entered the wide main hallway. I found my classroom, which was the last room on the left.

As I entered the empty classroom, my shoulders sagged. Maybe I'd actually get a few seconds to myself. Back home, I was always in my room and only came out when absolutely necessary. I'd only been here one day, and the constant swarm of people was getting to me. I'd figured coming here would be an adjustment, and that was just part of it.

I tossed my trash in the garbage can and headed to the back where I liked to be. This classroom was set up the same way as the one upstairs, so I took a seat and leaned my head against the dark gray wall behind me.

A few people trickled in but didn't sit near me. I'd never understood why, but most people kept a decent amount of distance between themselves and me as though they sensed something weird inside me, or maybe I had a resting bitch face. That seemed plausible too.

Even before my dad's death, I hadn't felt like I fit in with anyone until that day on the beach when I'd met the boy. For the first time in my life, something had clicked. Between losing that connection and my dad within a day, I couldn't breathe when I thought back on it. I had no clue why all of this was bubbling to the surface. Maybe it was because I'd gotten away from Mom and Sarah.

Something inside me shifted as heavy footsteps entered the room. My eyes opened, and there stood Golden Eyes. His attention was locked on me as he made his way toward me.

Every time I'd read a book where a character caught their breath, I'd laughed. Like, how did one actually do that? Did they stop mid-breath or maybe look constipated? But now I understood it. Every part of my body was focused on him and couldn't expend any extra energy beyond that.

"Hey," he rasped as he somehow fit into the desk beside me.

Any other guy would have looked ridiculous squeezing into something that small for them, but he looked damn sexy. The worst part was that I was noticing and couldn't stop.

"Hi," I said, forcing the word out.

He scanned my books on the floor and frowned. "Where's your backpack?"

"Oh." That snapped me out of my stupor. "It broke this morning," I said, lying through my teeth.

Egan's face wrinkled like he smelled something bad.

Dear God, please tell me I didn't fart. I'd have noticed if I had, right? I was tempted to sniff the air to see if I could figure it out, but I had already embarrassed myself enough.

"Well, why don't we go to the Student Center and buy you a backpack after class?" He smiled like it was the best idea he'd ever had.

What was it with him and wanting to buy me things? That wasn't normal, was it? "No, I'm good. I can probably fix it. No need to waste anything that can be fixed." That would be another item to pick up while I was out.

He pinched the bridge of his nose as it wrinkled.

Okay, I had to know. "Do I smell bad or something?"

A girl sitting at the front of the class looked back at me. Her low-cut red top left little to the imagination, and I probably would've been able to see her vagina in that super-short skirt if she hadn't been wearing tights due to winter. Her cinnamon-colored hair fell across her shoulders as her ebony eyes landed on me. "If you have to ask, it probably means yes." She patted the seat next to her and did a duck face while looking at Egan. "You can come sit next to me. I promise I don't smell."

"I'm pretty sure skanky stinks too." It was one thing when people talked shit about me behind my back, but when they were blatant enough to do it to my face, I had to put an end to it. Otherwise, I'd be bullied my entire existence. "And I'm sure if anyone gets within a foot of you, they risk getting an STD."

Egan's eyes widened, and his lips mashed together, but he couldn't hide the shaking of his shoulders.

"You bitch." The girl jumped to her feet like she thought she could do something about it. Her platform shoes had heels that were over six inches tall.

All I needed to do was break a kneecap, and she wouldn't be able to stand on the other foot or crawl back to her dorm. "Maybe." It was true, and even though everything inside me told me to put the girl in her place, I already made a big enough scene. I was tired of people shitting on me. Still, I didn't want to become like Sarah.

"Listen here." She stomped her foot like it didn't make her look like a toddler throwing a tantrum. "You're the one who said it. I just agreed and gave him another option."

Egan shifted in his seat, and I turned toward him, not able to hide my surprise. Was he really going to go sit next to her after offering to buy all of these things for me? Maybe he was looking for a lay.

Leaning over the desk, he arched an eyebrow and looked me directly in the eye as he responded to the girl, "There is no other place I want to sit than back here. I want to make that perfectly clear."

My blood pumped, and my body warmed. What the hell was wrong with me? I had to be falling sick or something.

I didn't know how to respond, and for a second, it felt like he and I were the only two people in the room. None of this made sense. He seemed familiar, but I'd remember someone like him. He'd be impossible to forget.

The professor entered the room and cleared her throat, forcing me to come back down to reality. While I'd been distracted by this guy, the classroom had completely filled, and she began class.

THE ENTIRE TIME IN CLASS, I tried to keep my eyes forward and on the whiteboard, but I couldn't repeat a damn word that the professor said. I kept wanting to look in Egan's direction. At one point, I stole a glance, which was a huge mistake. He was staring at me, and I wasn't sure if I should be thrilled that he was struggling too or scared that he'd caught me.

After class, I'd be going off-campus. I needed to run errands, but it was so much more than that. I had to reflect on what was going on with me. It was unnerving.

Class ended, and I stood, wondering if the girl would try to start shit with me again. Luckily, she darted out, eager to leave. At least, that problem was solved.

I heard Egan climb from the desk beside me. I'd taken a step toward the door when his sexy voice called out, "Hey."

The smart thing would have been to pretend I hadn't heard him, but my feet stopped.

CHAPTER FIVE

I hated the hold Egan had over me. Whenever he spoke, it affected me in forbidden ways, especially since I'd only met him yesterday. It warned of an unhealthy dose of attraction. I waited for him to finish whatever he wanted to say.

He moved closer to me and ran a hand through his hair. "Maybe after my next class, we could grab lunch together?"

"I don't date." I cringed at how he might take that. "Or sleep around."

Oh, crap. What if he hadn't meant as a date but as friends? No one like him would actually want to date me. He looked like all the statues of gods that littered textbooks —chiseled abs visible through his shirt and bulging every-where else ... and I meant *everywhere* else. My eyes almost flicked to his crotch. I lost all sense around him.

"Okay, good to know." He chuckled, but the smile didn't reach his eyes. "And that's too bad about the dating thing."

My heart picked up its pace. It had to stop doing that. "Really? You want to date me?"

His smile turned into a sexy smirk. "Why wouldn't I? You're beautiful, strong, and stand your ground."

I almost corrected him. I wasn't strong; I was scared. There was a huge difference, but for him to call me beautiful had caught me off guard enough that I was speechless. I welcomed it for a minute because, at least, I wouldn't babble something else embarrassing. "No, you're beautiful." Scratch that. There it was.

"I'm beautiful?" His eyebrows shot up as his forehead creased with confusion or surprise.

Right now, there was a fifty/fifty shot it could be either emotion. "God, no."

Startled, he tilted his head. "No?"

"I mean ... you're sexy." I needed to shut up, pronto. "Dead sexy." My mouth wouldn't quit, meaning there was only one thing left to do. I turned and ran out the door.

Dropping Spanish, or never leaving my dorm room again, wouldn't be a big deal. Both were viable options.

In the hallway, a large, warm hand gently grabbed my arm and turned me around. Tingles ignited from where his skin touched mine. He was so tall I had to lean my head all the way back to look into his eyes; otherwise, I'd be staring at his nipples. I bet guys didn't like that any more than girls did. Granted, his chest was pure muscle and no fat. I was tempted to reach out and touch it to confirm it'd be hard against my fingertips.

His eyes glowed. "You finding me dead sexy is a good thing."

The fact that I wasn't more freaked out by his glowing eyes and that I actually found him hotter petrified me. Something was broken in my brain, and I had to get my hormones under control. "I've got to go." The longer I stayed, the worse it would be. It took every ounce of willpower I had, but I pulled from his grasp and rushed back down the hallway. I needed fresh air.

Right before I turned to head out of the building, I glanced over my shoulder, worried and excited at the possibility of him chasing me. However, he stood right outside the classroom, watching me go. A frown marred his gorgeous face, and it bothered me that I'd put it there. I wanted to go back and make it right.

Instead, my survival instincts kicked in, reducing the urge, and I headed outside. I'd planned on going back to my room and changing to look for a job, but I needed a second to collect myself. The woods called to me. Maybe nature would help settle me.

No one watched as I broke through the tree line. At first, the trees were spread apart, but the deeper I walked, the more clustered they became. Growing up, I'd hang out in the neighborhood woods every Saturday morning when Sarah would leave to run errands or meet up with someone. It was the only thing that had kept me sane.

Hiking had quickly become my favorite pastime, and as I walked deeper into the woods, the burn in my legs brought relief. My arms grew heavy from the books I carried, so I found a bush to stash them in. A thirty-minute hike should snap me back to myself.

Sunlight trickled through the trees, casting long shadows in certain areas. Moments like these brought me peace. I never challenged why. Maybe it connected me to my father because we used to go on short hikes together.

With each step, my body warmed until I no longer felt cold. A slight breeze picked up, blowing my hair out of my face. The ground became an incline, forcing my calves to work even harder.

Even though the trees were bare, birds and squirrels

scurried from branch to branch. The chirping and rustling were like music to my ears, which most girls found strange.

As a kid, I'd believed I was connected to nature. I'd declared to Dad that I could shift into an animal if I wanted to. He'd laughed and asked me which one. I remembered pointing to myself and sticking my chest out proudly, saying, "A unicorn." His response had been perfect, especially for a little girl.

He'd replied, "If anyone could ever be a strong, powerful unicorn, it's you." Those words had made me so happy.

Of course, I wasn't a strong, powerful unicorn, and boy, had Sarah enjoyed teaching me that hard lesson. At first, I couldn't defend myself, but after years of martial arts training, I'd gained the skill and confidence to stand up for myself. And I'd defended myself one time. Sarah had cried out, alerting Mom. Mom had come upstairs, and my aunt had pointed out how I'd hurt her. Seeing my mom's disappointment had devastated me. I never defended myself again until yesterday.

A branch snapped a few yards away from me, and I stopped, scanning the area for anything out of place, but nothing stuck out, except for the silence.

All of the happy animal noises were gone, which meant a predator was out. I hadn't even considered a wolf would be out here, but I should have. The hundred and fifty acres of woods that surrounded the college had drawn me here. With that much land, large predators were a given.

My breathing quickened, and I turned around in place. I tried moving slowly and silently even if it was futile. Wolves had excellent hearing, but I hoped it was a different hunter that didn't have such enhanced hearing and sight. Moving slowly was my best option.

I put one foot in front of the other. Luckily, the way back was downhill, which would help me move a bit faster.

With each step, I prayed I put more distance between me and whatever was back there. The back of my neck tingled again just like this morning. It was probably my paranoia and nothing more, but if something was chasing me, it could be gaining ground, and I wouldn't know.

God, I'd been stupid to come out here alone. I should've known better since I didn't know this area. The real kicker was the fact I could be out here dead for days before someone even missed me. Maybe a professor would follow up with the business office to see why I'd missed class, or parts of my body would show up on campus from whatever animal had killed me. It really proved how alone I was in this world, and for the first time, I regretted it, which was strange. Normally, I didn't care, but now, it made me sad.

Another branch snapped behind me, closer than before.

No. Something was hunting me. There was no question now.

I took off running, acting like the prey it wanted, but dammit, I didn't care. Maybe its instincts to hunt and kill would drive it crazy and I could outthink it. Hunting was ingrained in whatever was chasing me.

In other words, I was dead.

Every rational thought left me, and I ran harder than I ever had in my entire life. The leaves crunched underfoot, telling the animal where I was going.

But I couldn't stop.

Something made a noise behind me, but I couldn't make out what it was, and I refused to turn around. It would only slow me down, and I was hell-bent on getting back to campus—hopefully in one piece.

My feet slipped on the leaves, and I slid a few inches before landing hard on my knees.

More noises came from behind me, and I couldn't help but turn around. Pure terror coursed through my body, and when I didn't see anything behind me, my fear went into overdrive.

Whatever was chasing me didn't want to be seen until it was ready. It would be less terrifying if I knew what I was up against, not that it would make a bit of difference.

I jumped back to my feet and took off again, running a tad slower. If I kept falling, it would take me longer to get back. Every few feet, I heard another noise. The predator was having fun and closing in.

The realization that I wouldn't make it back to campus slammed into me.

No, I couldn't give up. I'd risked it all to get away. I couldn't let it end just when I'd gained my freedom. Renewed energy invigorated me, and I kept steadily on my feet.

A low chuckle filled the air.

A fucking chuckle.

I didn't know of one damn animal that could laugh. A person couldn't be hunting me, right?

If so, they were a sick psycho. Now I couldn't force myself to look ahead. I needed to know what was behind me. I ran haphazardly forward as I looked back, and I slammed into something hard. As I bounced off, strong, solid arms wrapped around my waist, and I screamed louder than I had in my entire life.

My knee instinctively slammed upward, and a loud groan vibrated from his chest. This guy was huge.

As he crumpled to the ground, one hand released me to

cup his balls. Using that in my favor, I punched him in the face. Something popped, and pain coursed down my arm.

Of course, it would be some douchebag guy, but how the hell had he circled in front of me?

"Stop, please." The too familiar, sexy-accented voice groaned. "I didn't mean to scare you."

"Egan?" Wait … there was no way it could be him. I'd left him behind at the school. What was he doing out here? I stepped back so I could see him.

His face was red and scrunched in pain. "Yeah."

"We've got to go." He didn't need to be here. Now we'd both get eaten alive.

"What's wrong?" He straightened and looked behind me. "Did something happen?"

"Something is chasing me." My voice shook with fear, but I didn't care. "We need to go. We both could be in danger now."

"No, it's fine," he said as he placed his hands on my shoulders. "You're safe."

What was crazy was that I actually felt that way, but I didn't want to analyze those feelings, not after what I'd just gone through. "How do you know?"

"I just know." He sighed. "Stay right here and let me go take a look. I'll be right back." He stepped in the direction I'd been running from, and I grabbed his hand.

"Don't." I didn't want him to get hurt. "Let's get back to campus."

He shook his head, ready to argue, but I didn't want him to leave my side.

I pressed, "Please."

Something softened in his eyes. "Okay," he said gently. "I won't leave you."

I exhaled a breath I hadn't realized I'd been holding. "Thank you."

"Of course." He looked deeper into the woods one last time before turning and standing close to me. "Why don't we head back to campus and get you settled?"

"I'm all for that." Words had never sounded sweeter.

We trekked back toward the university in silence. A few minutes in, Egan looked at me and asked, "Why did you come out here all alone?"

"Wait ..." That reminded me... "I thought you had a class right now." He'd asked me to go to lunch in an hour.

He chewed on his bottom lip. "I saw you head out here, and I came looking for you."

Wow. He really was a nice guy. For some reason, that made this all worse. "You missed your class because of me?"

"It was just the first class to calculus." He waved his hand dismissively. "I took it last semester for a few weeks, so I already know the material."

"Oh." I guessed that made sense. "Did you drop it?"

"Yeah, something came up, and I had to leave." He shrugged as he looked at me again. "So I'm back and retaking the same classes."

He obviously didn't want to tell me more, and I wasn't one to push. God knew I had my own secrets. "Well, I hope everything is okay now."

"It is." He grinned. "What about you?"

We were getting closer to campus, and the bush where I'd put my books came into view. "Oh, this is my first semester at college." I didn't have too much to share.

At the bush, I stopped and grabbed my books.

He held his arms out. "Here, I can take them."

I almost handed them to him before I stopped myself.

"No, I'm good. Thanks, though." He'd saved my life. Every time I was around him, he took care of me in some way.

Something fell behind us, and I spun around. At least, we were close to campus. "We better go. That's what was going on earlier."

"Head back." His shoulders stiffened, and he grew rigid. "I'll be right behind you."

"I'm not going without you." Was he crazy? I couldn't leave him alone out here.

"Fine." He waved me on.

I took off running back to campus. After I'd run about a hundred yards, I realized I didn't hear Egan behind me. I stopped when more noises sounded several feet to my right. There was more than one predator. We were so screwed.

CHAPTER SIX

I wanted to yell for Egan, but that would only put us both in more danger. Maybe he'd heard the person and was hiding. I wouldn't blame him. After all, people only looked out for themselves. Since I was already at risk, it was my turn to protect him. "Who's there?" I dropped my books and spread my feet shoulder-width apart, crouching into a fighter's stance. Whatever it was could likely kick my ass, but I wasn't going down without a fight.

Footsteps approached me from behind a tree. I sprang into action and reached for whatever it was. My hand touched smooth skin, freaking me out, and I jerked the person toward me, prepared to knee them in the face. A flash of rose-gold hair flashed.

Sadie yanked her arm from mine and dodged my knee. It should have been impossible, but she moved fast.

"Jade." She stood and lifted her hands. "I'm not here to attack you."

"Then what are you doing out here?" None of this made sense. First Egan and now her. "I could've hurt you."

"I heard a noise and thought someone might be in trouble." Sadie gestured to the tree line several feet away. "But apparently, all I did was scare you."

"You shouldn't be out here." I snatched my books from the ground and glanced over my shoulder again. Egan was still missing. "But thanks for checking on me." I turned to go back deeper into the woods when Sadie grabbed my arm.

"I shouldn't be out here, but you're about to run back in there?" She shook her head and tugged me to the tree line. "Nope, that's not how this goes. You're coming with me."

"But ..." I tried to pull out of her grasp, but she held on firmly. I really wasn't getting out of this situation without causing a big scene. I didn't have much of an option, and after what I'd seen of her, I had a feeling she could kick my ass. "Okay." I sighed. "I'm coming."

"Good. You can join me and the girls for lunch." She continued to tug me toward the buildings. "I'm supposed to meet with them now."

"Uh ... I've got errands to run." Being around them didn't sit well with me. I didn't feel comfortable around others.

"Come on." Sadie stopped and turned to me. "You almost messed up my face. The least you can do is eat lunch with me." She pouted.

"You're manipulating me." For some reason, I didn't mind.

She pointed at herself and winked. "I'm not even going to deny it."

If I told her no again, she wouldn't push it, but after what I'd experienced in the woods, maybe it wouldn't be so horrible to make friends. I didn't have to get close to them or anything. "Fine."

Her mouth dropped. "Really? I figured you'd say no again."

"Oh." She hadn't expected me to say yes. "I totally don't have to. I really do have errands to run."

"Nope." She smiled, and it even reached her eyes. "You already said okay."

"Technically, I said fine begrudgingly," I teased, which surprised me.

"It's a form of yes." She looped her arm through mine and tugged me toward the Student Center. "And there are officially no take-backs."

Being around her felt easy when she wasn't having elusive conversations with other people. I wasn't sure how she would be around the other girls. "I can't stay for long."

"Middle ground." She nodded. "I can handle that."

We walked toward the Student Center in amicable silence. My thoughts kept going back to Egan, but I had the odd feeling he was all right. *How the hell could I know that?*

We walked into the building, and Sadie zeroed in on her friends all the way in the back corner of the over-crowded place. I could barely make out Roxy, but it was like Sadie knew where her friends were. It was strange, unless those were their normal seats.

She dragged me with her, and we squeezed by various tables to get to the booth. The two darker-haired girls sat together while the vibrant redhead had a vacant seat next to her.

The two girls sitting across from Roxy each had a travel cup and no food, while Roxy held two plates that each contained a double cheeseburger and fries. Roxy put one plate down in front of the open seat beside her.

All three girls glanced at me periodically, making me feel extremely paranoid.

"Thanks," Sadie said as she snatched a chair from a

vacant table and put it at the end. "There, you can sit here, Jade."

At least I wouldn't have to stand here awkwardly, pondering my next moves. "I'm going to grab a bite."

"Okay, we'll be here." Sadie smiled and bit into her burger.

I placed my books on the table and hurried away. When I stepped into the cafeteria, my heart calmed. I hadn't noticed, but adrenaline still pumped through my body from whatever had gone down in the woods. At times, it had sounded like an animal, but at other times, it had sounded like a person. It couldn't be both, so what the hell was it?

Scanning the food stations, I made my way over to the cheap chicken nuggets and fries baking under a hot lamp. They looked like they'd been out there a while. The chicken looked shriveled, but it was the cheapest food they had here. After packing a container and picking up a bottle of Coke, I quickly checked out at the register and headed back over to the four girls. They stopped talking as I approached, making me feel uncomfortable.

I quickly sat down and shoved a nugget into my mouth.

The girl with brown hair smiled. "Hi, I'm Katherine. I don't think we've met yet."

"No," I said around a mouthful of food. "We haven't. I'm Jade."

"I don't think any of you have met her," Sadie jumped in. "That's Lillith," she said, pointing to the darkest-haired girl. "And that's Roxy."

"Nice to meet you." I pretended not to know any of their names.

"Sadie was telling us she found you in the woods." Roxy took a sip of her water. "What were you doing out there?"

That was kind of odd and random. "Just needed to get away, so I went for a hike."

"Those woods aren't the best to go in alone." Lillith lifted her drink. "Last semester, a few people went missing in there."

After what I'd experienced today, I wasn't surprised. "Yeah, there was something out there. I have no clue what, though."

"You heard something?" Sadie frowned. "No wonder you were about to break my face." She chuckled.

"Yeah, it sounded like something was chasing me." And here I'd thought I was paranoid. There was no telling what had happened there. "A friend found me but didn't follow me out."

"That had to be scary. Where did your friend go?" Katherine asked with concern.

"I don't know. Egan told me to head back to campus, but when I looked back, he was gone." Talking about it had made me lose my appetite. Maybe I shouldn't have left him.

"If I know Egan, there's nothing to worry about." Sadie patted my arm reassuringly. "He has an uncanny way of always coming out on top."

Of course, they'd know him. "You know him too?" I shoved a fry into my mouth, trying not to let my insecurities bubble to the surface. When I imagined the type of girl meant for Egan, Sadie popped into my mind.

"Yeah." She smiled. "We all started here last semester together. He was in a class of mine."

I wondered if they'd ever dated and tried pushing it from my mind. It didn't matter.

"So, where are you from?" Roxy asked as grease dribbled down her chin.

"Ew." Lillith grabbed a napkin from the holder and

threw it at her. "Leave greasing up for the bedroom and just verbal details for me. I don't need a visual."

Oh my God. They were going to talk about sex with me here. Hell, I didn't even know how to do that. I'd never even kissed a guy. Okay, that was a lie. I'd kissed a guy when I was thirteen, but there'd been so much slobber involved that I did my best to forget it.

"Most of the time, my mouth isn't involved unless he's been extra good." Roxy wiped her face with an exaggerated motion. "And that doesn't need greasing up." She wiggled her eyebrows.

I choked on my food.

"Aw, you're embarrassing her." Lillith tsked. "You should really learn when to keep your mouth shut."

"Oh, bite me, va—" Roxy's eyes widened, and she stuttered. "You meanie."

Katherine glared at Lillith. "You started it."

"Whose side are you on?" Lillith stuck her tongue out at her friend.

"The right side." Roxy motioned to herself. "Which is also known as Roxy's side."

"Just ignore them." Sadie turned toward me and rolled her eyes. "Those two like to give each other a hard time. It's the foundation of their friendship."

That was clear and amusing to listen to. I'd bet those two never let things get boring.

"Hey." Roxy wrinkled her nose. "Don't tell our secrets."

Lillith snorted. "I agree. I don't like being called out."

Katherine lifted her cup. "Yet you two are the first to call anyone out."

Roxy's forehead lined. "What's going on here?"

"I don't know." Lillith pouted. "But I'm thinking we need to do something."

"Please don't." Sadie shook, feigning horror. "We don't want to scare Jade off after just a few minutes."

"Fine." Roxy flipped her hair over her shoulder and smiled at me. "Only because she seems cool."

Now *that* made me feel awkward, so of course, that meant my mouth opened. "So what, are you two on a diet or something?" I glanced at Lillith and Katherine, who only had drinks.

"Oh ..." Katherine grimaced.

"No, we aren't," Lillith interjected and ran her finger along the top edge of her lid. "We just enjoy drinks with lots of protein."

I hadn't heard of that, but to each their own. I finished the rest of my food and glanced around. The place had become even more packed. "Well, thanks for letting me join you all, but I'm going to get going." I needed to find a job. The food here was more expensive than I'd realized.

"No more going into the woods alone, okay?" Sadie narrowed her eyes at me, driving home her point.

"Don't worry, that won't happen again."

"What's your number?" Roxy asked as she pulled her phone from her pocket. "We can bug you later about dinner."

They actually wanted to be my friends. I rattled off my number and waved, turning to the door.

Outside, a cool breeze lifted my hair, and my eyes instinctively went to the woods. Egan stepped out of the tree line. He wasn't injured. The only thing different was that his perfectly styled hair was messy, adding to his allure.

His attention remained firmly locked on the woods, and the other two guys from the bookstore the other day stepped out and talked to him.

At least, he wasn't alone.

My body wanted to go to him, but I'd been around him enough for one day. I forced myself to turn toward the dorms and took off without looking back. It was probably one of the hardest things I'd ever done.

In my dorm room, I breathed a sigh of relief. Vera wasn't there, so I'd actually have a moment alone. Setting the books on my desk, I flopped onto the bed and removed my cell phone from my pocket. I unlocked it and searched for places that looked promising to work.

The best establishments were upper scale, but not too uppity that only the rich could afford. It still shocked me that the rich were usually the worst tippers. They'd order multiple bottles of hundred-dollar wine but leave a ten percent tip.

One place caught my eye—Haynes Steakhouse. The restaurant was located only ten minutes from here, making it an even better option if they were hiring. I hoped they didn't ask for references, but I'd figure that out later.

I stood, grabbed my black slacks and white button-down shirt from the closet, and quickly changed. I put on some mascara and nude lipstick to look a little more professional. Now it was time to go since the restaurant was open for lunch.

I PULLED into the parking lot of the older building with new charcoal-blue siding. There were two dark, cherry wood doors right in front with a bronze sign displaying "Haynes Steakhouse." Mercedes-Benzes, BMWs, Lexus, and other high-end cars were in the parking lot, and my crappy car definitely looked out of place. I parked in the parking lot farthest from the door, underneath a tree, praying to God that the people inside wouldn't notice my car.

Grabbing my wallet, keys, and phone, I climbed out of the car and slammed the door. As I approached the entrance, a worker opened it, allowing me inside. A grin filled his face. "Welcome to Haynes Steakhouse."

"Thanks." I entered the building and walked up to the large cherry wood hostess desk.

"How many will there be?" a girl my age asked and picked up a few menus. Her amber eyes stayed locked on me as she turned toward the seats. Her white shirt and black slacks fit her like a glove, and her long, light auburn hair, pulled into a French twist, completed the look flawlessly.

"Actually, I'm hoping you all are hiring." At least, they didn't think I looked too underdressed to eat here. "I'm hoping to apply for a server job."

"Sure." She smiled and lifted a finger. "Give me one second, and I'll get the manager. He just got here. I'll be right back." The girl walked away, leaving me alone.

The restaurant had booths along the walls and several tables scattered throughout. The place was packed, but the seats were spaced out enough that it wasn't overwhelming. The tables and chairs were made of dark maple and covered in thick white tablecloths.

This place wasn't as nice as the one I'd worked at back home, so hopefully, the tips would be better.

The hostess reappeared with a man only a couple of years older than me. When his eyes landed on mine, warning and dread filled me. A smirk lifted his lips, and everything inside me told me to leave.

CHAPTER SEVEN

"Here she is, Ollie." The hostess waved at me. "She wants to apply for a server role. I wasn't sure if we're hiring."

"We just had an opening come up," he replied, and a chill ran through me. With each step, his golden-brown hair bounced, and his cognac eyes scanned me. He was taller than me by a couple of inches, making him around six feet tall.

"Who quit?" she asked and placed a hand on her hip.

"Daryl," he answered distractedly, his focus locked on me. "He turned in his notice last night."

This line of work had a high turnover rate. That was one reason I wasn't too worried about finding a job.

"And," he said, snapping his fingers, "I happen to have time for an interview."

"Really?" Her brows furrowed, and she glanced back toward the kitchen. "I thought there was an issue going on."

"It's fine." Ollie gestured for me to follow him. "I can make time for this."

Maybe this had been a mistake, but I couldn't turn

down an interview. Perhaps the guy was awkward like me, and that was what was putting me on edge. I needed the money, so I obliged and followed him to the very back of the restaurant where no one sat.

"It's after the lunch rush, so we can have some privacy back here." He walked to the booth along the back corner wall and pointed for me to sit across from him.

Pushing away any doubt, I followed his instructions and sat at the table. The only thing that prevented me from standing and running out the door was that I could hear people walking by. This section was close to the kitchen, so if I needed to scream, someone would hear me.

He held out his hand over the table toward me. "I'm Ollie. And you are?"

"Jade," I said breathlessly but loud enough for him to hear. I had to become more confident or I wouldn't get this job. "I'm Jade," I said louder. When I touched his hand, it was cold and clammy, and it took everything in me not to jerk my hand back.

"Nice to meet you, Jade." He leaned back in his seat, the corners of his mouth tipping upward like there was a hidden joke I wasn't privy to. "Are you looking for a full-time position?"

"No." I hadn't even considered they'd want someone full-time. "I'm looking for a part-time job. I'm a student at Kortright University and need to work evenings or weekends."

"Good." He placed a hand on the table. "We are looking for a part-timer to work during the dinner rush, so that's perfect. Friday evenings and the weekends are the busiest hours."

"That would be great." I wasn't sure if I should be excited. This whole situation seemed peculiar. "I served at an upscale Italian restaurant back home, so I do have experience."

"Then you're hired." He lifted both hands and chuckled. "You sound like the perfect fit."

"Wait ..." I didn't want to discourage him, but he'd only asked me two questions. "Don't I need to interview with the other shift manager and fill out an application?" *Please don't ask for references,* I chanted internally. If Sarah went by my old workplace and Ollie called, she could find out where I was.

"I'm the manager over the weekend evening shift, so you only need to meet with me." He sounded so proud of himself. "And yes, I'll need you to complete an application, but it's just a formality for your paycheck. I'm assuming you can start Friday."

Thinking about my entire situation, I couldn't turn this down even if I'd wanted to. Any other place would have called my old job. "Sure. I can. Thank you."

"Of course." Darkness rolled into his eyes. "I need to help out a fellow classmate anyway."

That caught me off guard. "You go to Kortright?"

"Sure do." He tapped his fingers on the table. "I think I might have seen you on campus."

"Maybe." I didn't remember seeing him, but hell, I couldn't point out most of the students I'd seen today.

"Oh, I most certainly did." He leaned over the table. "I could never forget a face like yours."

I wasn't sure if he was being nice or hitting on me. Surely, with him being my boss, he was trying to be nice. "Is it your first year?" Changing the topic was my best bet.

"Yes, but I'm a junior." He leaned back and crossed his arms. "I transferred this semester since an interesting opportunity popped up."

"Well, a manager and a student." I had to admit, I was slightly impressed. "I bet that's hard to juggle."

"Nah." He shook his head. "I work the weekends and a few evening shifts during the week. It's not too bad, but I've always been ambitious."

"Good for you." I had no clue what to say. "Thank you for giving me this job. It looks like what I'm wearing is the standard uniform."

"Yes, another sign it was meant to be." He stood and pulled at his own white button-down shirt. "I need to get back. Tell Betty to give you the application on the way out, and just have it completed when you return on Friday. Be here at five sharp."

"Betty?" He'd have to give me a little more information than that.

"The hostess." He frowned. "Sorry I can't walk you out, but I need to return to the kitchen to ensure the problem was resolved."

"No worries," I said too eagerly. I just didn't feel comfortable around the guy. "Thanks again."

"Sure. I'll see you around." He chuckled as he stayed firmly in place.

I stood and forced a smile in return. "I'm sure you will." I stepped away slowly, ensuring that I didn't run to the door.

As I turned the corner to the hallway, I looked back at where we'd been sitting, and he was standing there, watching me walk away. It unnerved me.

My pace quickened, and by the time I reached the hostess desk, I was faintly out of breath.

The girl smirked. "Are you okay?"

"Yeah." I sucked in a breath and got my act together. "Ollie told me to get an application from you."

"Really?" She shrugged and pulled a drawer open. She snatched a paper and handed it to me. "There you go."

"Thanks," I said and headed for the door.

Outside, a tingling feeling ran down my spine. It was similar to what I'd felt in the woods earlier today. I tried to brush it off as I rushed to my car, but the feeling only intensified. I glanced over my shoulder at the restaurant, but there was no one but the doorman near a window, and his attention was firmly on his phone.

I wondered if my imagination had gotten carried away earlier today in the woods. There was zero reason for me to be feeling this way. I was in a small, bustling, picturesque town. It wasn't like something could get me.

I tried to appear calm, cool, and collected as I walked to my car. If any regular customers or coworkers saw me acting strange, it would make my first few days of work that much harder. I didn't need to be labeled a complete outcast. At work, I needed to be friendly so people would cover for me if I needed to run to the bathroom.

My hands shook as I pulled the keys from my back pocket and went to insert them into the lock. Having a nicer car with keyless entry would really come in handy right about now. My hands jerked, making the key scratch the handle, and some of the paint flecked away.

Dammit, something had to give.

Something hit the ground right behind me, and I jerked in that direction. My heart hammered as I saw a twig not even a few inches from me. I glanced up at the tree I was standing under. Dear God, a twig had scared me.

I'd never been like this until yesterday. It had to be stress or my mind playing tricks on me. I hadn't run away to lose my mind. I had this.

Turning back to my car, I held my hand steady and

unlocked the door. Mind over matter. That could be my new motto until whatever this was settled down.

My urge to jump into the car and get the hell out of here surged, but I'd expected it. I climbed into my car and shut the door, proud of myself for not slamming it. I started the car and pulled out like a normal human being, but when I pulled onto the road, I stomped on the gas pedal, my instinct taking over.

I ARRIVED BACK at school close to five. I'd stopped at Walmart to pick up a few things, only to realize I couldn't afford more school supplies and a backpack until after my first night of tips. I'd settled on picking up a jacket, some granola bars, peanut butter, and bread to get myself through the rest of the week. Those weren't my favorite things to eat but having money for gas was more important.

I found Vera sitting at her desk as usual. She chewed feverishly on her lip as she read.

When I shut the door behind me, she jerked her head up and slammed the book.

"Sorry." I hadn't been silent when I'd entered. "I didn't mean to startle you."

"No, it's fine." She waved it off like it was no big deal. "I was just caught up in the book."

The book she'd been reading was bound in leather. "Wow, that looks like an old book."

"It is." She opened the desk drawer and placed the book inside. "It's my grandmother's journal. She left it to me."

That sounded strange, but who was I to judge? "That's nice."

I placed my bags on the desk, and she wrinkled her nose.

She stood and glared at the bags. "Please tell me you aren't planning on eating in here."

"No?" I hoped this was a trick question and she was messing with me. Otherwise, I'd be taking my peanut butter and bread down to the lobby to eat. I wasn't sure if that option or the Student Center was worse.

"Thank God." She sighed, clearly relieved. "I was worried for a second."

Wow. I hadn't pegged her to be worried about eating in our room. "Nope, no problem here." But I was willing to do whatever was necessary for us to get along. My stomach rumbled, which was perfect timing. I didn't want to be up here much longer anyway.

"On that note, I'm going to go eat." I pulled out a plate from the small package of paper plates, the jar of peanut butter, a couple of slices of bread, and a plastic knife. "I'll be back shortly."

"Take your time." She sat back at her desk and pulled out a textbook. "I'm going to get on my homework."

She had homework already on her first day of a new semester. Neither of my classes did. Maybe she was taking harder courses. I walked out of the room and took a deep breath. The lobby had been pretty empty, so now would be the best time to eat before it got busy.

The hallway was deserted, so I made my way to the elevator and pressed the button. Within seconds, the door opened, revealing Sadie, Roxy, Lillith, Katherine, and the teal-haired girl from class earlier.

Roxy's eyes zeroed in on my bread and peanut butter, and her mouth dropped open in horror. She breathed, "For the love of God, tell me that isn't your dinner."

I stood there and blinked in response. Her reaction baffled me.

"Oh, stop." Katherine rolled her eyes as she lifted the hand holding her coffee cup. "Peanut butter is a staple in the American diet."

"Everyone needs meat." Roxy grabbed my arm and pulled me inside the elevator. "Please tell me that's just a snack."

"No?" That was the second time in less than five minutes that I'd answered in the form of a question. "It's my main and only course."

"I don't eat meat," the teal-haired girl responded. "Not everyone does."

"That's because you are ..." Roxy paused like she was searching for the right word.

"Unique," Sadie blurted, clearly uncomfortable.

Her awkwardness made me laugh. "Didn't I call you that earlier?"

"Yes, you did." Sadie laughed, returning to her usual demeanor. "I guess I can't give you hell about that any longer."

I turned my attention to the drinks the two dark-headed girls carried. "You're drinking coffee or protein again?"

"Protein." Lillith lifted the cup to her lips and took a large gulp. "It never gets old."

The elevator opened again, and I stepped off first, heading to one of the vacant couches.

"Where do you think you're going?" Sadie asked as she caught up to me.

"My roommate doesn't want me eating in the room, so I'm stuck down here." I raised the food. "This is where I'll be eating my dinner."

"Nope." Sadie shook her head. "No one is meant to eat alone. Join us."

"Nah." I was tempted to go, but it was better that I hang out with them in moderation. Besides, they were only asking because they'd seen me. "You all go and have fun. I don't want to impose."

"How are you imposing?" Roxy's forehead lined with confusion. "If anything, we should be hurt."

"What?" Her words made no sense. "Did I do something?"

"Yeah, you ignored my texts." Roxy tapped her foot. "For a peanut butter sandwich."

She'd texted me? I set the plate on the couch and pulled out my phone. Sure enough, I had a text asking if I wanted to join them for dinner.

"Now you have no excuse." Lillith snatched the plate and headed to the door. "You're stuck with us."

They were putting so much effort into inviting me that I couldn't say no. "Fine, but only because you're all so desperate for me to join." I grimaced, realizing what I'd said.

Roxy burst out laughing and wrapped an arm around my waist. "You'll fit in just fine."

We walked into the Student Center, and my eyes darted to Egan and his two friends sitting in the middle of the seating area with several tables pulled together.

"And there is my sexy man," Roxy said to me and pointed right at the buzzed-haired friend.

Holy shit. They really were friends with Egan. I had to get away.

CHAPTER EIGHT

W hen the girls told me they knew Egan, I hadn't expected this. But as I pieced together their comments, it made complete sense. Of course, this would be their group of friends. The guys looked strong, sexy as hell, and commanding. They'd want girls like them beside them. I wondered which one was dating Egan. My gut said Sadie. "Oh, I didn't know you were meeting up with more people." I couldn't watch him fawn over someone. It would bother me. "I'll just head back to the dorm."

"Nope." Roxy tightened her arm around me. "You, dear girl, are stuck with us."

As she dragged me over to the table, Egan walked over to Sadie. The buzzed-haired guy raised an eyebrow but didn't say anything.

"Here, let me help," Egan said as he took my plate from her hands and headed back to the same side of the table but two spots down from the guy with the tribal tattoo at the end. He placed the plate in front of the chair right next to himself.

Strange, I thought Lillith had been carrying it. I guess that just proves my focus was off, again. Ugh.

The tribal tattoo guy chuckled. "You think that bread will fill you up?"

"Stop." Lillith pursed her lips. "He's always been a gentleman. Don't give him hell because you two act more like apes."

"Oh, please." The buzzed-haired guy motioned to the chair next to him and pointed at Roxy. "Just taking care of my girl."

Roxy bounced over and kissed his lips before sitting down. "Now, go get me food. I'm hungry."

"Come on." Sadie tugged my arm and sat next to the guy with the tattoo, leaving me to sit between her and Egan. I wanted to remain standing, but that would make this worse. There had to be a way out of here.

The other chairs filled in with Lillith and Katherine sitting in front of Egan and me and Roxy across from Sadie. The teal-haired girl sat at the end between the two guys.

"This is Jade," Sadie introduced me to the two guys. "This is my boyfriend, Donovan." She faced him with an adoring smile. "And that is Axel."

"So the girl who burned Egan officially has a name." Axel placed an arm around Roxy's shoulders. "I'm hoping to see more instances like that occur."

"Burned Egan?" Roxy arched an eyebrow. "What haven't you told us?"

I wanted to die. Coming here had been a huge mistake. "It was nothing." I placed the jar of peanut butter and the knife on the table.

"Doesn't sound like nothing." Lillith leaned across the table. "Spill."

"She's obviously uncomfortable," Egan said with annoyance. "Why don't you cut her some slack?"

The table went quiet as everyone's attention landed squarely on Egan.

At least, it wasn't on me. I opened the jar and spread some peanut butter on the bread, wishing to hurry and eat.

"And you said he was a gentleman," Sadie joked, eliminating the awkwardness from the table.

"I'm going to go grab something to eat." Egan turned to me. "Do you want anything?"

"Nope." A bottled water would've been good, but he'd already done enough for me. I could choke down the bread. "Thanks."

"Okay," he replied and walked toward the cafeteria, leaving me behind with everyone pretending they weren't staring at me.

Sadie turned to Donovan and smiled sweetly. "Mind getting me a Philly steak? That way I can stay here with Jade and protect her from these vultures." She waved her hand from Lillith to Katherine to Roxy.

"I may be many things, but I'm no damn bird." Roxy harrumphed and crossed her legs. "I'm almost offended by that."

"You'd have excellent vision." Katherine sipped her drink. "So, it wouldn't be horrible."

"My vision is amazing enough already." Roxy stuck her tongue out at her. "And I'm thinking red wouldn't be a good color for feathers."

Lillith bobbed her head. "Red's not a good color for anyone."

"I think her hair is pretty," the teal-haired girl interjected. "There are many people back home that would kill for hair like that."

"See?" Roxy smirked. "Naida knows how it is."

How the girl had referred to her home made me curious. "Where are you from?"

"F—" She began.

"Finland," Roxy interrupted. "She's from Finland."

"Really?" She had an accent, but not one I'd expect from there. "That's neat. I've never been anywhere but the southeast." One day, I hoped that would all change.

"While you ladies gab, we'll go get some food." Donovan kissed Sadie and looked at her adoringly. "One steak sandwich coming up." He turned to Naida. "Your usual?"

"Yes, please." She smiled genuinely. "Thank you."

The two guys walked off, and Roxy's focus landed on me. "What's the story with you and Egan?"

I should've known she'd be like a dog with a bone. "It wasn't a big deal." It really was a big deal to me, but if they knew that, then they really wouldn't drop it. The five girls' faces wrinkled like they smelled something disgusting. I sniffed, trying to figure out what the hell it was, but I didn't smell a damn thing. "What's wrong?"

"Nope." Roxy pointed at me. "Not happening. Don't change the subject."

"I was short on cash while buying my books, and he happened to overhear and helped me out." I left out the part where he'd been perfectly fine getting all of my books. What kind of guy did that?

"Whoever winds up with him will be one lucky lady." Lillith almost purred. "Sexy, kind, and an overall good guy."

I wanted to slap her hard. The overwhelming urge caught me off guard. I had to stay away from him.

"Hey." Katherine's brow furrowed. "We aren't trying to upset you."

"Oh, I know." I was acting irrationally. So what if Lillith wanted him? If they were single and wanted to ... I couldn't even get myself to say the word internally. But I couldn't have him. "I'm not upset."

Sadie covered her nose with her hand and winced. "Stop pestering her."

"What did you do?" Egan asked, sliding into the seat next to me. "I thought I told you to leave her alone." Protectiveness laced each word.

However, I couldn't focus on that. Egan had brought back two trays overflowing with food. He had a little bit of everything—pizza, hamburgers, pasta, a few desserts, and two drinks. I moved my plate toward Sadie to give him more room.

He picked up one of the cups and a wrapped burger and handed them to me. "I hope you like Dr. Pepper and hamburgers."

My stomach rumbled even though I'd eaten a peanut butter sandwich. It smelled good, but I needed to save my money.

"Wait." Roxy narrowed her eyes as they flicked from Egan to me. "You're sharing your food?" She stood and reached over to grab a fry.

Right before her hand got near one, he smacked her hand away. "I'm sharing it with her, not you."

"I'm fine." If I got too hungry, I'd go out in the hallway and eat a granola bar. "I don't need your food." He must have thought I was a charity case. That had to be it.

"Nope, I got too much." He winked and nodded to the burger. "We don't want it to go to waste."

I should've argued more, but it smelled way too good. "Thank you." I wouldn't even pretend I'd pay him back. I barely had enough for gas before Friday.

A huge smile spread across his face. "You're welcome."

Avoiding everyone's gazes, I kept my eyes on my burger and took a bite. Blissfully, the other two guys came back.

I remained quiet for the rest of the time, trying to process why I felt so drawn to the sexy man beside me.

BY THE TIME I finished the hamburger, Egan had put a piece of apple pie in front of me. For the first time in a while, I was stuffed. The others were chatting and having a good time, and I enjoyed listening to the back-and-forth banter. Every few minutes, one of them would glance in Egan's and my direction like they were trying to figure out something. I wanted to tell them, "So am I," but that would have made this situation more uncomfortable.

I crumpled up my wrapper and stood. Now was the perfect time to run away. "Well, thanks for letting me join you all tonight, but I'm going to head back to the dorm and call it a night."

Egan stood and picked up both trays. "I'll walk you back."

His attentiveness stunned me. Sure, he'd asked me out earlier, but when I'd turned him down, I'd figured that would stop his attempts. "It's fine. Stay here with your friends."

"Not after what happened in the woods," he rasped and stepped toward me. His citrus scent filled my nose, causing my brain to short-circuit. I nodded before I even realized what I'd done.

"Good." He took my wrapper from me and threw away the trash on the tray.

Concern flashed across Katherine's face before she smiled. "We'll see you later."

"Yup." I needed to get away from all of the awkwardness. "See ya." I rushed to the front of the Student Center without waiting for Egan. The more I was around him, the more I lost my head. I pushed the door open and stepped outside.

Even though the group had been nothing but nice to me, I'd felt every one of their glances. Egan's attention had them focusing on me even more.

The door swung open, and a sexy, deep voice called out, "Hey, wait up."

"Look." I had to end this now. I kept my back to him, not wanting to see his reaction. If he looked relieved, it could really hurt me. "I don't need your pity."

"Is that what you think this is?" He gently grasped my arm and spun me around. His head jerked back like he'd been slapped. "That's not it at all."

"You paid for my books and now my dinner." I sucked in a breath, forcing myself to loosen the grip I held on my pride. "I really do appreciate it, but I'll be fine. I don't want you to feel obligated. I can take care of myself."

"Of course you can, and there is absolutely no reason to pity you." His eyes locked on mine. "I know it sounds crazy, but all I want to do is take care of you."

"Why?" I asked before I could take it back. My body was on alert, desperate to hear his reasoning.

"There's something about you." He cupped my cheek and looked deeply into my eyes. "Something I can't and don't want to shake."

The gold in his eyes lightened, and the stubble on his chin reflected the moonlight. He licked his lips, and I wondered what they tasted like.

Everything inside me wanted to kiss him. I stood on my tiptoes as his head lowered, feeling our connection too. My heart pounded in my ears, and my stomach roiled with anticipation. Right when his sexy, full lips were inches from mine, my brain screamed.

I was here to get an education and make something out of my life. Not piss it away on a guy. I shoved him away, pushing him off balance. He hadn't expected that.

"No, I can't do this. I'm sorry. Please don't follow me." I turned and ran toward the dorm, hoping he'd respect my wishes. When I didn't hear his footsteps, I breathed a sigh of relief and glanced over my shoulder to find him watching me. A frown marred his face, and so much hurt wafted off him that I could even feel it. I hated that I'd done it, but I couldn't turn out like my mother—barely surviving.

As I opened the door, he turned to go back inside the Student Center and rejoin his friends. I watched him disappear inside, tempted to rush back to him, but I wouldn't do that. I couldn't afford to be stupid and become more broken than I already was.

A cry for help pierced the air, coming from near the library. After another moment, a girl screamed again, "Please don't!"

I took off running in that direction. I couldn't let someone get hurt when I could hear them. No one else was outside or within hearing distance.

I ran as fast as possible and stopped by the library building. I had no clue where the scream had come from beyond there. I stood still, trying to pick up cries, heavy breathing, anything.

But I heard nothing. "Hello?"

A bird took off from the woods, flying high into the sky. Something dripped from its beak and left a trail behind.

I rushed over to the liquid, pulled out my phone, and turned on the flashlight. I stuck my finger in the warm liquid and placed it under the light. My heart sank, and I gagged.

It was blood.

A whole lot of blood.

Enough for a thick trail to be left behind.

What the hell kind of bird was that? "Is someone here?" An eerie feeling overcame me as I slowly followed the trail of blood. Surely, a bird hadn't caused the girl to cry out.

I wiped my finger on the grass, desperate to get the blood off me. It could have come from anything. Even after the blood was gone, I could still feel it. I needed to wash my hands, but first, I had to make sure someone didn't need help.

Following my gut, I pulled myself together and proceeded toward the tree line. When I reached the first line of trees, I stopped. I wouldn't be making the same mistake in complete darkness.

Hands shaking, I used my phone to cast a light on the ground. A cold breeze picked up, chilling me to the bone and making the situation even scarier. I took several steps, scanning the area for something out of place, but nothing showed.

Maybe someone was playing a joke, or the scream hadn't come from this direction. Standing out here in the cold wasn't smart. I had to get back inside. But when I took a step back toward the dorm, the blood trail popped back into my mind.

I'd missed something.

When I spun back around and lifted my phone, my light shined a little farther back, and my blood turned to ice.

CHAPTER NINE

N o. There was no way this was happening. I screamed, unable to process what the hell I was seeing.

A girl I'd never seen before lay on the ground, dead. But that wasn't the worst part. Something had pecked out her eyes and not delicately. They'd gone deep, and blood still trickled from the wound.

Throwing caution to the wind, I moved to go inside the woods, but strong arms that were already way too familiar wrapped around my body and turned me around, burying me into a hard chest. I hadn't realized I was crying until his hands were rubbing my back as I sobbed.

"Hey, it's okay," Egan said comfortingly. "It's going to be okay."

"No, it's not." Even though I no longer faced her, the image had been burned into my brain. "I think she's dead. We need to check."

Footsteps rushed over to us, and Donovan said, "Why don't you take her away from here? Axel and I can handle this."

"Handle this?" I pulled away from Egan's arms and

glared at him. "You mean call the cops, right?" Hysteria bubbled through me. "She is a person."

"Yes, we're going to call the police." Donovan lifted a hand. "I just meant you can go back to the dorm."

"But I found her." The police would want to question me. "I can't leave."

Axel ran toward the girl and stopped short of her. He faced us. "She's dead."

"How the hell do you know?" I marched over to the girl, pushing by Axel, and dropped to my knees. "You have to check for a pulse." I placed my fingers on her neck. There was nothing, but her skin was still warm to the touch.

If I'd only gotten here a few minutes earlier ... I wrapped my arms around myself, and tears fell to the ground.

"Guys," Donovan groaned. "Get her out of here."

Hands scooped me off the ground and cradled me against a warm chest. I almost fought against him until the citrus smell slammed into my nose.

It was Egan, not Axel, but I hadn't heard him walk over, and he must have moved super-fast. I glanced into warm, golden eyes. I was losing it. "I need to stay."

"They'll tell the police where to find us," Egan reassured me as he walked out of the woods toward the library. "We'll just sit at a bench outside of the Student Center."

He really wasn't giving me much of a choice, and I was too tired to try to get out of his arms. My emotions rolled inside me like tumbleweeds in the desert.

"Let me know if you need anything," Egan murmured.

I closed my eyes and cuddled against his chest. My brain yelled at me to stand on my own feet, but I pushed the voice away. There was no other place I'd rather be.

His heart beat steadily, calming mine inside me. I'd

never felt so safe in my entire life, and for once, I allowed myself to feel it. I couldn't be strong on my own right now.

"Is she okay?" Sadie's concerned voice startled me.

Again, I hadn't heard anyone approach. I lifted my head to find Sadie and the other four girls standing next to us.

"She's—" Egan started.

"I'll be fine," I cut in. I wouldn't allow them to treat me like I wasn't there. I might not want to stand on my own two feet, but I wouldn't be ignored.

"Says the girl being held," Roxy snorted.

"Well, if you'd just stumbled upon a girl with her eyes pecked out, I bet you would be a little unstable too," I snapped back, ready to defend myself.

"What?" Katherine's mouth dropped open, but her reaction fell short. "You saw what?"

"People don't just stumble upon death like that." Naida pursed her lips. "It's not something they're used to."

See, she got it. "Thank you. Each one of you would be struggling too if you were in my position." I smacked Egan gently on the chest and pointed to the ground. It felt imperative that I stood. "The death is a lot easier to process when you're not the one who saw all the blood."

"You're right." Sadie glared at her friend and gave me a friendly smile. "I'm sorry you saw that. Is there anything we can do?"

"No." Egan shook his head. "Donovan and Axel are handling it while Jade and I hang out here to wait for the police."

"Okay." She glanced at her friends and sighed. "You have our number if you need anything. We'll head back to the dorms."

"I'll keep this," Katherine said, lifting my jar of peanut butter, "with us for the night."

Oh, damn. I'd forgotten it when I'd been desperate to leave Egan behind. I kept being an ass to him, but here he was, treating me great. I wasn't sure what to make of it. "Thank you. Just make sure you don't get tempted to eat it due to your all-liquid diet."

Lillith laughed hard. "We will try our best, but no promises."

The girls headed back toward the dorm.

Now that we were alone, I felt awkward. He'd seen me have a complete meltdown. He must have been ready to get the hell away from a train wreck like me. "Look, I'm sorry."

"For what?" He took my hand and tugged me over to the bench. We were the only two out here, most likely due to the chill in the air. I hadn't been able to get a jacket before the girls had pulled me from the lobby, so my teeth rattled together.

"It's cold out here." He scooted closer and wrapped an arm around my shoulders, pulling me into his side.

The warmth coming off him comforted me. "How are you so warm in just a dress shirt?" I'd bet my skin was cool to the touch.

"It's all the fat." He glanced down at his stomach. "It keeps me insulated."

"There is not any fat on your body." The memory of him carrying the box sprung to mind. I'd seen the outlines of everything he had to offer. "So that can't be it."

"You've looked?" A smile tugged at the corner of his mouth as his eyes ran over me.

This would have been the perfect opportunity for me to stay silent. "It's hard not to." My breath caught on the last word. He was damn sexy, and he had to know it.

Now, I wanted to die. My cheeks had caught on fire.

He brushed a fingertip across my cheek. "I'm glad because you're extremely beautiful and sexy."

Sexy.

No one had ever called me that before. Sure, a few guys had called me pretty in passing, but that was it. Sexy was a whole different caliber than I was. "Thanks." I bit my bottom lip and stared at the ground.

This was wrong. A girl was dead, and here I was, getting all swept up in a golden-eyed god.

He must have realized where my thoughts had gone because he pulled me even closer against his chest. "I'm sorry about tonight."

"Me too." The image reappeared in my mind. "I still can't get over it." I probably wouldn't get any sleep tonight. "I heard a cry for help, but I didn't get there in time." That made me wonder. "How did you find me?"

"I heard the scream too." He sighed and ran a hand through his hair. "I wish I could've gotten there first. It would've been nice for me to find her and not you."

"Nice?" That sounded like the wrong word to use.

"Okay, maybe not nice." He blew out a breath and lowered his forehead against mine. "But I would've preferred it. You should've never seen that."

"And you shouldn't have either." Being with him felt so natural. We'd only met yesterday, and not under the best circumstances, but I felt like I'd known him my whole life. "Unfortunately, we both saw it."

"I hate to ask." He cupped my face. "But did you see anything?"

"You wouldn't believe me." I still had a hard time processing it.

"Try me."

"Okay." I pulled back to gauge his reaction. "When I

got to the woods, a bird flew out with blood dripping from its beak." My gaze went straight to the finger that had touched the blood.

He remained stoic. "Any clue what kind of bird?"

"I'm pretty sure it was a falcon." I tried to recall the bird. I'd been locked on the liquid since I hadn't expected it. "It had all white feathers underneath because the light from my flashlight app reflected off it clearly, and dark gray on top. Part of it blended in with the darkness."

"Well, it's not here now." He looked skyward, searching for the threat. "And you're safe."

He actually believed me. "I've never heard of a common bird doing something like that."

"Me neither." He frowned like he knew something that I didn't before he sighed. "Maybe it had rabies."

"Really?" That was a stretch, but I didn't have any better ideas. "Do you think the cops will think I did it?"

"No." He shook his head. "You had only left moments before from a crowded Student Center. You'll be fine."

I hadn't thought of that. It was a damn good thing I'd gone with them. Imagine if I'd stumbled upon her and no one had seen me.

I laid my head on his shoulder, enjoying his closeness. The silence descended between us, and fatigue hit me hard. The horror I'd witnessed had taken a lot out of me. I breathed in his unique scent.

His cell phone dinged, startling me.

He huffed, "I'm sorry." He pulled the phone from his pocket and glanced at the text. "The police want to talk to you."

"Okay." I was ready to get it over with.

My alarm blared, waking me. I blinked, trying to figure out where the hell I was. Last night was a huge blur, and I'd dreamed about it all night.

I sat up, and the familiar bed and sleeping roommate made things click. I was back in my dorm room.

Now that my brain was working, I remembered Egan walking me to my room after the police had dismissed me as being traumatized. They didn't believe the bird story and told me the coroner would figure out a more plausible explanation. Egan had stood protectively over me and shut the police down when they'd become condescending. For the first time ever, I'd let someone take care of me. When he'd walked me to my room, he'd reassured me and kissed my forehead. I never would've believed a man like him could exist.

Vera rolled over and glared. "Turn that blasted thing off."

"On it." I sat up, grabbed my phone, and turned it off.

"Why are you taking such early classes." Vera propped herself on her hand. "Who was the guy last night, by the way?"

"Oh, his name is Egan." I couldn't believe I'd managed to sleep, but his presence made me feel calm. I'd been so tired I hadn't changed out of my clothes. "Sorry about passing out on you last night."

"You were out." She snorted, which oddly fit her. "I don't think I could've woken you if I'd banged on drums."

"I'm sorry about that." I'd barely been able to talk when the exhaustion had hit. I'd wanted to sleep and not think about the bird and the girl anymore. "I saw something that took a lot out of me."

"Oh, what?" She sat up in bed, her attention fully on me. "Did something happen?"

She hadn't said more than a handful of words to me, and now she was acting like we were best friends. She had watched me last night, but I hadn't cared. Ever since coming here, I'd felt like I'd entered a whole different dimension. "I found a girl dead in the woods. Her eyes were gone."

"Yikes! The university sent a letter out about it last night." Vera shivered. "I didn't realize you were part of the group it referenced."

I didn't have much to say in response, so I grabbed my towel and headed to the door. Her morbid curiosity had gotten to me.

After getting ready, I left the dorm, munching on a granola bar. I'd been stupid and actually put makeup on in case I ran into Egan. At this rate, there was no stopping me. The one thing I hadn't been able to buy and bring to the dorm was a coffee pot, so I rushed into the Student Center to get a cup. The place was packed with everyone whispering about the dead girl. Despite them whispering, they might as well have been screaming in my ear.

I felt the need to get away as the images of last night flashed inside my head. I hurried to the cashier, threw five dollars down, and didn't wait for the change. I couldn't afford it, but I didn't care.

Outside, I inhaled and slowed my pace. I didn't want people to think I was stranger than they already believed. I headed toward Grey Hall and stayed on the sidewalk, passing the woods. Part of me wanted to go inside to see if I could figure out what was out there hunting, but a larger part of me was in survivor mode. I didn't need any more trouble than I'd already found.

But the *kak, kak, kak* of a falcon call caught my attention. I turned my head, and a bird flew out from the trees.

Then it stopped and hovered in the sky. Its round eyes locked on me, and I stopped in my tracks.

My body froze when I noticed the crimson dot on the pure white feathers under its beak.

The bird and I stared at each other for God knew how long until it swooped down, heading directly at me.

CHAPTER TEN

I stood frozen in disbelief. The entire world had gone insane. A fucking bird was attacking me. It was close enough that I could hear its feathers against the wind. I needed to duck, but I was entranced. All I could do was stare at the blood spot. It had to be the same bird from last night.

"Jade!" Egan called out, and I heard footsteps pounding in my direction.

He wouldn't be able to reach me in time, but his words snapped me out of my mental fog.

The falcon was only two feet away when I tossed my coffee and books at it and hit the ground. The bird dodged everything, buying me time to crouch.

A large body shielded me, easily covering all of me, and I knew exactly who it was. But how had Egan reached me in time? He had sounded several yards away.

Another round of *kaks* came from the bird, close at first, then sounding farther and farther away. There was definitely something wrong with that damn bird.

"Are you okay?" Egan slowly moved off me and sat on the sidewalk in front of me. "Did he get you?"

"He?" Out of everything that had happened, only I would focus on his mention of the bird's gender. "How do you know it's a he?"

"Intuition." He surveyed my body for any injuries. "Are you hurt?"

"If my pride counts, then yes." A stupid bird had taken me down. "What the hell is wrong with that thing? Someone needs to shoot it." I didn't usually advocate for killing, but that bird was an exception.

"Don't worry." Egan stood and held his hand out to me. "I plan on handling it."

"You're good with guns, eh?" There probably wasn't much he wasn't good at. Of course, that put my mind right in the gutter. "Are you okay?"

"Not so much guns, but I can fend for myself." He kept his hand extended, waiting for me to take it. "And yes, I'm just glad I got to you in time."

Not wanting to be a jerk, I grabbed his hand, and something shocked between us where our skin touched. The jolt was strong but not unpleasant. Once I got to my feet, I pulled my hand away and wiped it on my jeans. "Thanks." It still tingled from where we'd touched. It had to be static electricity. That was the only thing that made sense.

He bent down and scooped up my books, frowning at my coffee cup; the lid had popped off, its contents staining the white sidewalk. He sighed. "It looks like we need to go get you another coffee."

The thought of going with him was alluring, but I had a class to get to. "Thanks, but I'll be late." I stepped closer to him without meaning to. His body drew me in, and the overwhelming urge to touch him rocked through me.

"Then let me walk you to class." He turned toward Grey Hall. "I can carry these for you."

"Okay." The words were so soft he might not have heard them, but his responding smile told me otherwise.

We walked toward the building in amicable silence. Just being beside him brought me peace, which bothered me again. Last night had been a moment of weakness, and look at what happened after I let my guard down a little—I desperately wanted to be beside him. He was consuming way too many of my thoughts.

He held the door open for me, and I slipped inside, heading through the main corridor to the hallway. My class was on the first floor and midway down. I stopped and held my hands out, ready to take my books from him. "Thank you."

"Anytime." His eyes landed on my lips.

My brain screamed at me to go into the room, but my body refused to budge. "Thank you for that out there." He'd protected me once again.

"You don't need to thank me." He pushed a piece of my hair behind my ear, and a jolt warmed my body. "I'll always protect you." His words were a promise, and I liked them way too much.

He didn't remove his hand, and it felt like we were the only two people in the world. His touch felt good, and I found myself stepping into him. Damn traitorous feet. My eyes flicked to his lips, and I licked mine, wondering what he tasted like.

"You can't always protect me." I laid a hand on his chest, feeling his hard muscles. It felt like a spell overcame me as the jolt connected us, making me crave him even more. "You can't be around all the time."

His lips were only a few inches away. "I can try." His

breath hit my lips, and I closed my eyes as I rose onto my tiptoes.

His lips touched mine gently, and a shock like I'd felt between our hands hit me hard between our lips. It hurt but in a pleasant way, and I almost moaned. He tasted of vanilla, which caught me by surprise, and I never wanted to taste anything else ever again. The thought startled me out of the moment.

No, I couldn't get attached to a man. Not like this. In just two days, I'd felt things for him that should've been impossible. If something happened to him, it could break me like my mother had broken when Dad had died.

Some say she'd survived my father, but not in a healthy way. Sarah had sucked her into their unhealthy, codependent relationship, and Mom had never been the same. I didn't want to become like that.

I jerked away and shook my head. "I'm sorry." I spun and entered the room, leaving him behind.

THE ENTIRE TIME in both classes, my mind kept replaying our kiss. I couldn't pay attention to either teacher. The connection between us was indescribable, which meant we couldn't do this any longer. Our relationship would only end with one or both of us getting hurt.

I walked out of my chemistry class and outside Webster Hall. The all-brick building was my favorite. Though similar to the others, it was a little larger because of the science labs. This building had four stories and a slanted roof. From the school's website, I'd read that it had been built between the times of Wilson Hall and Grey Hall.

No stairs led up to the double wooden doors, and more

people were heading into this building than the others. People's bags bumped into me as I hurried to the courtyard outside the Student Center. It wasn't quite as packed here since there was still a chill in the air.

Desperate to get back to my dorm, I picked up my pace, ready to lose myself in a good book or show.

As I passed by the Student Center, I noticed Egan's large frame standing in front of the girls' dorm. He stood there like he was waiting on someone. I both hoped and dreaded that it was me. And that was the crux of my problem.

Dang it, I didn't need to run into him. I had to avoid him. His presence made me do stupid stuff.

I kept my gaze down, but I felt the moment his eyes landed on me, almost like they were part of me, and it petrified me. At the split in the sidewalk, I cut toward the library about ten feet from him and walked faster.

"Jade!" he called out, fracturing a piece of my heart.

This was not normal. Getting this emotionally involved with someone in such a short amount of time wasn't rational. If this wasn't the first sign of a very unhealthy relationship, I didn't know what else was. It already felt like the only way to find peace was to be near him.

No, I couldn't do this. His footsteps pounded on the pavement, catching up to me. He grabbed my arm, gently turning me around. Eyes locked on me, he asked, "What's wrong?"

"I ..." I'd never had to say such hard words before. "I need space."

He blew out a breath as he flinched. "What? Why?"

"It doesn't matter." I decided to escape before I caved. I had to protect myself. "Please, give me space." I jerked my arm out of his hold and ran, refusing to look back. My heart and body screamed, but I ignored them, pushing through. In time, the pain would ebb. It had to.

THE NEXT TWO weeks flew by in a blur. I worked the busiest shifts at Haynes Steakhouse and made pretty decent money. Ollie was as strange as they came, but he mostly left me alone. I got there when it was busy and left around midnight, completely exhausted after cleaning up.

A few more deaths had happened on campus, but luckily, I hadn't stumbled upon any of the bodies. Everyone was on edge because some of the victims had had their throats cut. I'd thought this place was supposed to be a safe haven, but apparently, something similar had happened last semester. People had gone missing and were never found. This time, dead people were being found all over the place.

When I wasn't working or in class, I hid in my room like a coward. I even tried hiding from Sadie and the other girls. They were a little more persistent. One night, they'd forced me to hang out in one of their rooms, promising that Egan wouldn't show up. The first time Roxy had brought him up, I'd gotten up and left. I knew where their loyalties lay, and they weren't with me.

For once, Vera sat up instead of bitching about my alarm. That was unusual.

"You okay?" I asked.

"Oh, yeah." She yawned and closed her eyes. "Just going to the library this morning for a paper due in Composition II."

"Considering how much you read and work, I'd think it'd already be done." Every time I walked in, she was usually reading her grandmother's journal or a textbook of some sort. "I don't know how you can fit so much in and still have more to do."

"There's a lot more to studying than just the basics." She flipped her long hair over her shoulder and stretched. "Besides, it's not just school work I want to focus on. There's a lot about me you know nothing about."

That was fair. "Got it. Well, I'm going to go get ready for classes." This conversation was already awkward, so I wanted to escape quickly.

"Whatever happened to that guy?" she asked as I gathered my things.

She must have meant Egan. "Nothing. We just haven't been hanging out." Each day, staying away from him got harder instead of easier. It was ridiculous and didn't help that he sat beside me in Spanish class. I'd see him watching me out of the corner of my eye, and it would thrill me. He looked as miserable as I felt.

"He seemed into you." She pulled the covers off her legs and placed her feet on the ground. "And he's hot. I was hoping you'd be dating and he might have a brother."

Okay, that shocked me. We barely talked, and now she wanted to double-date with me? "Uh ... no clue if he has a brother." There were so many things I didn't know about him, and her question added to my curiosity. Damn her.

"You're really going to let a guy like that pass you by?" She reached for her thick glasses on the nightstand and placed them on her nose. "I get we aren't friends, but you're my roommate. I want the best for you."

"Thanks." I grabbed the rest of my clothes and opened the door. "I really appreciate the concern, but I'm good."

I stepped into the hallway, and right before I shut the door, Vera yelled, "Someone else will get his attention if you keep acting like that."

The door closed behind me, but I couldn't move. It was like I couldn't even fucking breathe. The thought of him with someone else hurt. How had I let this happen?

It didn't matter. I repeated the phrase several times, but my heart screamed in protest. It did matter, and I wasn't sure what to do.

Needing to get outside and clear my head, I quickly showered and got dressed. I foolishly put mascara and lip gloss on because it was Friday and I'd see him. I'd been doing so well until Vera had put those insane thoughts in my head.

I rushed back into the dorm room and grabbed the new black backpack I'd bought after my first weekend working. It'd been a godsend, not having to carry all my books around while people gave me strange looks. Vera had left, so I didn't have to deal with any additional awkward conversations.

Throwing my bag over my shoulder, I strolled over to the Student Center, grabbed my standard cup of coffee, and put in the cream and sugar. Something tickled at the base of my neck. Almost every day, it felt like someone was watching me, but I'd never felt it in here. I turned around, but like every other time, nothing was there.

At first, I'd assumed it was my aunt, but now I needed to admit I was paranoid. I wondered if anything had actually chased me in the woods that day. Brushing it off, I rushed to class, eager for the weekend.

I WALKED INTO SPANISH 101, and Egan was already there. I hated when he got there first because he'd watch me the entire way to my seat. At least, when I beat him, I could have my book pulled out, pretending to read.

As I settled into my seat, his attention stayed locked on me. He always made me feel like I was the only person in the room ... like I was special.

While I leaned over to pull my book from my backpack, he leaned toward me. The edge of his shoulder touched the front of mine. The jolt sparked between us even through our clothing. I couldn't be the only one feeling this ... could I?

Trying to pretend I hadn't noticed anything, I sat up and opened my binder. I took out my pen and tapped the paper over and over again. Nervous energy ran rampant in my body.

He scratched the back of his neck and cleared his throat like he was about to say something.

No, he couldn't talk to me now. I still wasn't strong enough. I needed fate to intervene and help me stay strong.

The professor entered the classroom, saving me from talking to Egan, and I exhaled loudly.

She clapped her hands several times and smiled at us. "As you know, your first test is coming up next week, and one section will be on pronunciation. The best way to do well in this section is to practice speaking. I will pair you up with a partner to practice for the first twenty minutes."

Good, that meant I could turn my desk away from Egan. That would help some. At least, he wouldn't be tempted to talk to me.

As she paired off students and got closer to me, it became crystal clear that fate had a dark sense of humor.

"And you two," she said, pointing to Egan and me, "are a pair."

There was no getting around this. I would have to talk to him. I just hoped I could stand my ground.

CHAPTER ELEVEN

"All right." The professor twirled her finger around. "Get to work with your partner. Use the vocabulary words we've learned in the first five chapters."

I didn't move my desk; I was hoping this was all a bad dream. I'd been keeping him at a distance, and boom—just like that, it was over. Him sitting next to me had been bad enough, and now I had to talk to him. The more I saw him, the harder this all was.

The corners of Egan's mouth tipped upward, infuriating me. He scooted to the side and pushed his desk right next to mine so that his leg brushed against mine. The jolt between us was stronger than I remembered, stealing my breath.

Dammit, all of those feelings crashed into me, more powerfully than before, and my hand itched to touch him. The memory of how it had felt to have his hard chest pressed against mine and strong arms wrapped around me almost undid me.

How the hell was it possible? I'd kept my distance to prevent this exact thing from occurring. But the connection between us had strengthened, and I was at a loss as to why or how. Even the vanilla taste of his mouth flitted into my mind as his citrus scent surrounded me. My body buzzed with the need to feel more of him.

Him being so damn attractive made it harder to think straight. How could I be thinking about all the things I wanted to do with him right here in the middle of the classroom? It was so inappropriate, but I didn't care. I wanted to cave, but I couldn't.

"Hola," he rasped, adding to his damn sexy allure. "How have you been?"

"That wasn't Spanish," I bit, coming off like a bitch. Ugh, I didn't want to be like that, but my survival instincts had kicked in. "Muy bien, gracias."

"Look, I know we need to study, but can we talk for a second?" Egan leaned over his desk to catch my gaze. "I've been trying to respect your wish of needing space, but I don't understand what happened between us."

Me neither, and that was the entire problem. "We can't do this right now. We're supposed to be studying." If I let my grades slip, I would lose my scholarship, which was unacceptable.

"How about after class, then?" He rubbed a hand down his face and sighed. "At least, give me that. I want to make things right."

"Yes" almost formed on my lips, but I squashed it down. If I let him talk, I wouldn't be able to stay strong. "I'm really sorry, but there isn't much to say." I bit my lip, wishing he would drop it, but I was thrilled he hadn't. These conflicting emotions were wearing me out. "And right now, I really need to study. Please?"

He huffed, clearly disappointed, but nodded. "Okay." The hurt in his eyes bothered me more than I'd like to admit. But I focused on the task. It was the only way I'd come out of this unscathed.

I RAN out of Spanish class so fast it wasn't even funny. I didn't even pack my books. I grabbed my stuff and got the hell out before Egan could process what I'd done.

After dropping my books off in the dorm, I stayed in the room to get myself together, enjoying this rare moment alone. Since I took earlier classes, this was my little reprieve from Vera.

Once I got situated, I opened the window, allowing a cool breeze in the stuffy room, and took my phone from my pocket. I lay on my bed and logged into my Facebook Messenger account. That was the social media platform Mom used, and there were more messages from her. She begged to know where I was and to please come home. I'd broken down a few days after getting here and responded, needing her to know I wasn't dead.

I might have run away, but I still loved Mom.

We talked a little back and forth, but I limited my responses. I didn't need to accidentally drop a hint of where I was.

I made sure to never post anything and turned off the locator. I needed to remain hidden, but Mom had made it clear that Sarah was pissed and doing everything in her power to find me. The police refused to look for me since I was of age and was in contact with Mom. I wasn't a missing person, after all. So, that had been a relief.

When my stomach rumbled, I forced myself to my feet. I headed down to the Student Center to grab something to eat before Egan and his friends got there. The one time I'd gone through the line, Sadie had chased me out, trying to get me to eat with them. She'd frowned the entire time I'd turned her down. I needed to stay away from them since they were close with Egan. So, once again, I was utterly and completely alone. But it was for the best.

From outside my window, a familiar voice caught my attention. "What the hell do I do?" It sounded like Egan.

I peeked out the window and saw Egan sitting next to Sadie on a bench outside the guys' dorm. His hair was messy, revealing he'd run his fingers through it.

"I couldn't even go to my next class, Sadie." He lifted his head skyward. "She won't talk to me."

"She needs time," Sadie reassured him and patted his arm. "Remember how Donovan acted at first. Strong feelings like that are overwhelming."

Ugh, the fact she could tell how attracted I was to him further embarrassed me. I had to be drooling or foaming at the mouth whenever he was near.

"What if she doesn't feel it, though?" Egan's shoulders sagged. "Maybe my intensity is scaring her."

"You're being insecure. The way she looks at you proves she does." She dropped her hands into her lap. "And maybe you're being too nice."

Yup, there was my proof. She could clearly see my attraction to him, but who wouldn't find him sexy? He deserved someone not broken. The thought of him with someone else didn't sit well with me, though. Something inside demanded for that girl to be me.

"But she asked for space," he growled and glanced around to make sure no one could overhear them. "What kind of mate would I be if I didn't give her that?"

Mate? My heart dropped. That was either an odd way of saying "dating interest," or he viewed me as a friend. But if we were friends, would he be that upset about me not talking to him? I had to stop being stupid. I was the one who'd pushed him away, not the other way around.

I shut the window harder than I should have, but I was that damn desperate to not hear anymore. Everything inside me wanted to run down there and ease his pain. Stupid, sexy man with his god-like biceps and ample lips that I wanted to devour and ... Oh, dear God, I had to quit. If I kept going, I'd run down there and lick him like a lollipop.

Snatching a notebook off the floor, I used it to cool my ass down. I needed a cold shower before heading to work. I glanced at the clock and realized it was noon. At least, my homework would distract me now so I wouldn't have to do it later, and I'd eat another peanut butter sandwich since Egan was hanging out outside. It was time to get my act together and not obsess over the conversation I'd overheard.

I FINISHED PUTTING lip stain on my lips and took a step back. I'd been wearing more makeup to work, hoping it would increase my tips. I didn't know if it worked, but I earned more than some of the other servers.

The clock read three-thirty. I had only thirty minutes to get to Haynes. Given how reliable my car had been lately, I might need every second.

Outside, dread pooled in my stomach. My eyes darted to where Egan and Sadie had sat a few hours before as if I still expected them to be there. Each day, my paranoia increased, and I had no clue why.

The weird feeling tickled down my spine. I spun around and found nothing out of the ordinary. A *kak* sounded nearby, indicating a falcon was near. I swore that sound followed me wherever I went. Even at Haynes, that damn bird followed me, but there was more than one falcon in the area, so I was just being hyper-sensitive to them since that night. A shudder rocked through me every time I remembered.

I ran to my car, unlocked it, jumped in, and peeled out of the parking lot. My poor car sounded like it was dying, but I didn't let up. I would outdrive that bird.

I got to Haynes several minutes early, which was what I liked. I hated arriving right on the minute. If you pushed being right on time and something went wrong, you could easily be late. I entered the bustling restaurant. The older crowd always came in first, followed by the younger customers.

I passed by Betty and waved as I rushed to the back to get my apron and notepad. A few servers stood in the back, talking as one shift changed to the other. The room was smaller, so I squeezed between a few people and grabbed the black apron.

"Hey, Jade," Michael called as he walked up to me. "You're taking over my section." His shaggy charcoal hair hung in his eyes, emphasizing his ice-blue irises. He was a couple of years older than me and always nice.

"Got it," I said and held my hand out.

He handed over the paper with his open orders and smiled. "There's a party tonight if you wanna meet up after your shift."

This was the second time he'd asked me out, and I didn't know why, but it rubbed me the wrong way. "Sorry, not interested. We've been through this." If I were going to date anyone, the guy I'd choose was back at Kortright.

"Fine." He shrugged. "You can't blame me for trying."

"Yeah, I can," I said teasingly but didn't really care if it came off that way. He knew I was serious. "All right, let me get to work." I squeezed past everyone and turned toward the back section of the restaurant. I actually preferred it to the other sections. At the front of the building, near the hostess stand, it got a little chaotic once the waiting room got overcrowded. You'd have tables complaining about people hovering over them or their food and whatever else they could come up with.

As I stepped back into the hallway, that eerie feeling washed over me. I was getting so sick and tired of it. I turned around, expecting not to see anything, but I squealed when a thin frame hovered close by.

Instinct took over, and I grabbed the person's arm and punched him in the face. The guy's head flew back and hit the wall so hard it left a hole in the sheetrock. I turned to throw him over my shoulder and onto his back when the guy groaned, "God, Jade. Stop."

I paused and looked the guy in the face. It was Ollie. I dropped his hand and stepped back, asking, "What the hell are you doing standing in a dark corner like that?"

"I just got here and was looking to see who was on time." He stepped toward me, getting a little too close for comfort, and rubbed his jaw. There was a large red mark where my fist had connected with his face. Despite the pain, his eyes glinted darkly as he chuckled. "Why are you so jumpy?"

The asshole enjoyed scaring the shit out of me. He really was off his rocker. "Sorry for punching you." I'd needed to say it so I wouldn't lose my job. "But you caught me off guard."

"You've got strong instincts." He grinned, revealing yellow teeth. "That's good. It'll come in handy."

"Look, am I in trouble?" I gestured to the hole. "I can pay to fix that if it's any consolation."

"No, I'll handle it. After all, I scared you." He cleared his throat and smiled. "The way you rush around, I should've realized you'd startle easily. It doesn't help that so many girls are showing up dead on campus."

He always gave me the creeps. A rational person wouldn't stand there, smiling about dead girls. Each time I saw him, the worse the creepy feeling got. He didn't affect anyone else the same way, but I sensed a darkness around him I couldn't explain. He reminded me of my aunt when she was out in the real world. Somewhere deep inside, he was unhinged. "I don't rush."

"Sure." He lifted a brow and winked. "We can go with that."

Yeah ... creepier by the minute. "Okay, then. Sorry again." I took a few steps back, ready to get away. "I need to check on my table. See ya around."

"Be careful, Jade."

The words sounded like a threat, but I chose to ignore them. I had customers to wait on, and I didn't need extra drama in my life. Maybe next week, I'd look for another job after school. Getting away from him was becoming more and more of a priority. At least, my attack against him might make him think twice about stalking me.

I walked to the table, checked on their order, and got straight to work. Losing myself in orders brought me some comfort. Those types of conversations were easy. The customer would tell me what they wanted and what was wrong. There was no guesswork. As long as I did my job effectively and with a smile, I got paid and moved on to another set of customers. It was mind-numbing and busy.

Out of the corner of my eye, I saw Betty seat three

people in a middle booth. I dropped off the drinks at one of my tables and headed over to the new customers. When I approached the table, I almost stopped in my tracks. Sadie and Donovan were on one side, their eyes locked on the table, with Egan on the other side, smiling worriedly.

Of course, they'd be seated at my table, and I couldn't run away without causing a scene. Egan might just get his way and force me to talk to him.

CHAPTER TWELVE

"Hi, I'm Jade." I cringed internally, but I would be professional and play my role. "I'll be your server tonight."

"You work here." Egan sighed and closed his eyes. "Of all the places."

His reaction felt like a slap. He was usually so eager to talk to me, but it was clear he was less than thrilled to see me. "Not sure what that means, but okay." I tried to keep the hurt out of my voice. "So, what would you like to drink?" The quicker I could get their orders, the faster I could get away. I hadn't been prepared to see him.

"Egan?" Amber squealed from behind me. "Is that you?"

She was my least favorite coworker here. She wore over-the-top makeup, unbuttoned her shirt to give customers a peek of her cleavage, and flipped her hair so much I swore it had to be a compulsion. However, she was the only server who earned more tips than me.

Pushing past me, she slid into the seat right next to him,

and irrational anger overwhelmed me. That stupid bitch knew him. My heart sank. "You know each other?"

Egan winced, and his eyes locked on me. "I used to work here."

"And he disappeared right before we got to know each other." She turned to me, forming her dark red lips into a pout. Her moss eyes glowed with power like she knew this affected me. She flirted with everyone and competed with me for the most tips, but this was something more. She wanted to make it clear that Egan was hers.

"That's a bit of a stretch." Egan tried scooting away from her, but he was so large, and she'd basically sat right on top of him, so he didn't have much room. "We never even talked outside of work." His cheeks turned pink, and I wanted to snatch her by the hair and yank her away from him.

"Oh, stop." She ran a hand down his chest and purred, "You know we have unfinished business."

Sadie glanced at me with pure pity. "I'd love a glass of water."

"Same." Donovan tugged at the collar of his polo shirt. "If you don't mind."

"Got it." I kept my attention on them, refusing to look at Egan. If her hand was somewhere near his southern region, I'd come unglued, and that wouldn't be good for anyone.

"Why don't you get me and Egan here a few shots of whiskey?" She placed a hand possessively on his arm. "We can start the night early."

"I am actually here with my friends," Egan said.

"Don't worry." She giggled. "I don't mind." She turned her body into him. "I'll need to get to know them eventually."

Wow, this girl was more brazen than I'd thought. But

Egan wasn't trying too hard to tell her to fuck off. "If you want whiskey, you'll have to get it yourself." At least, she'd have to gain distance from him. "You may be off duty, but you're not twenty-one." I glared at her. "And I refuse to serve anyone underage." I spun on my heel and marched off to the kitchen, needing to catch my breath. I hadn't even asked if Egan wanted anything else to drink. For all I cared, he could drink his spit.

In the kitchen, I leaned against the wall and closed my eyes. I'd never felt this angry and out of control in my entire life. I didn't have a right to feel this way. I'd pushed him away, but it didn't matter. Seeing him with someone else highlighted the mistake I'd made. He couldn't be interested in her, but the words tasted bad in my own mind. Why wouldn't he be? She was gorgeous and into him.

I had to get out of there. I couldn't watch him show interest in someone else. I had enough money saved from the past few weekends to leave early tonight.

With a renewed goal, I went searching for Ollie. It was like the prick had disappeared.

A thin sweat broke out against my skin at the realization that I might not be able to leave and I'd have to watch Amber with him all damn night.

"Hey, are you okay?" Jerry, the assistant manager, stepped from the back of the kitchen, his brows furrowed. "You don't look so hot."

I didn't have to lie. My stomach was upset over it all. "I'm not feeling great, and I can't find Ollie anywhere."

"Yeah, I was looking for him too." He shook his head, causing the lights to reflect off his balding spot. "One minute, he was talking to me about the schedule tonight, and the next, he was gone. I'll split up your tables. Go home and get some rest."

"Are you sure?" It was a godsend that I'd run into him instead of Ollie. I had a feeling the actual manager wouldn't have been so nice. "I can try—" I prayed this didn't shoot me in the foot, but I had to pretend I hated to go.

"No, it's fine." His eyes warmed, reminding me painfully of my dad. I tried staying clear of him because of that. "Go on. You don't need to be serving food if you aren't feeling right. Let me know if you need anything."

"Thanks." I removed the apron and placed it on the hook. I drew the keys from my pocket and headed to the back door. I refused to give Amber the satisfaction of seeing me leave.

Outside, the tingling feeling hit me again. What the hell was going on with that? It didn't even register until I heard a noise behind the dumpster a few feet away. The disgusting smell of rotting food hit me, and I almost lost my lunch.

I had no interest in finding out what was making that noise, so I turned and ran out of the dark alley and toward a street light.

More sweat coated my body as I rushed around the side of the building and onto the grass that led to the parking lot. Right in front of the entrance, several large groups of people were waiting for a table, so I slowed down to appear more casual.

My head inadvertently turned toward the restaurant, and I searched for Egan. Obviously, I was a glutton for punishment, but it wasn't like I could see them. They were at the back of the building.

I wasn't sure which one was worse—seeing Amber draping herself over him or imagining what they were doing together right at this moment. I forced myself to focus on my car and tried to push him from my mind.

But I couldn't do it.

The way she'd run her hands all over him kept replaying in my mind. What kind of hussy did that? The kind that wasn't afraid to go after what they wanted. Someone completely opposite of me.

Maybe I was more like my mom than I liked to think. I was so worried about getting hurt that I was letting things fall through the cracks. But as long as he was happy, I figured I would survive.

I sobbed the entire way back to the dorm. Once I got into that room, Vera would probably pepper me with questions about him, and I'd have to hold myself together. I refused to appear weak in front of anyone. Showing weakness made you vulnerable, and when you were vulnerable, people took advantage of you. Case and point —Sarah.

My tires squealed as I pulled into my normal spot as far away from the buildings as possible. The car didn't necessarily embarrass me, but it stuck out like a sore thumb. I turned off the engine, unbuckled, and sat there for a moment. I wiped the tears from my cheeks and took deep, calming breaths.

They didn't work.

In fact, I only cried harder. The void deep within me got bigger. A piece inside me had always seemed cold. I could touch it, but it wouldn't warm no matter what. It'd been there for as long as I could remember, and years had passed since I'd thought about it.

No matter what, I would survive this. I refused to give in.

Minutes ran together as I allowed myself to break down for the first time in ten years. The last time I'd cried like this was on the day of my father's funeral. Little had I known that day would be the last one of my childhood. My life had changed the moment we'd gotten into Sarah's car to head back to live with her.

My body shook with emotions as I mourned the loss of not only my dad but my mother too. And of the sexy stranger I'd only known for a handful of weeks.

Someone pounded on my window, startling me. My head jerked left, and I found Egan staring right at me. His body sagged as he took in my state.

Embarrassed, I used the sleeve of my white shirt to wipe away the tears again. When I pulled it back, black mascara streaked it.

My eyes flicked to the rearview mirror, and I wanted to die. My worst fear had been confirmed. My eyes were red, and the mascara was smeared under my eyes. I looked like a damn raccoon.

"Jade," he said deeply. "Please unlock the door."

The way my name rolled off his tongue made my heart flip-flop in my chest. "I ..."

"Please," he said again. "We need to talk."

He was right, and I was being ridiculous. My refusal to get out of the car wouldn't prevent him from telling me he was dating someone else. And here I'd thought he'd been trying to talk me into seeing him while it had probably been about Amber the entire time. Gathering all of the strength I had, I unlocked the door.

"Thank you." He opened it and held it for me. "Are you okay?" He straightened, focusing on me.

"No." I didn't have the energy to lie. There was no point. I had to be honest. We deserved that. "I hope I didn't ruin your night with Amber." I wanted to spit her name, but I managed to only grunt it. The fact that I was being irrational pissed me off.

"That's what I thought this was about." He touched my

face, and our strange connection buzzed between us as tenderness reflected in his eyes. "You heard her. She hadn't seen me since last semester when I disappeared. She means nothing to me. I didn't go there to see her."

"Right, but you didn't seem upset with her lying all over you." Oh God, I had to stop. I sounded so pathetic.

"Jade—"

"No, it's fine." I pushed him away. It was time to remember this was for the best. "It makes sense that you'd be interested in someone else. Hell, we've only kissed once." Tears burned my eyes again. How the hell was there any liquid left in my body?

"Stop." He gently grasped my arm and pulled me out of the car and against his chest. "I will never move on from you."

"What?" I sounded stuffy, and I pulled back to look up at his face. "But you let her—"

"I shouldn't have." His forehead lined as he cupped my face. The jolt flowed between us. "She surprised me, and I didn't want to be rude. But I hurt you, and I wish I could undo that."

I nearly denied that he had, but that wouldn't accomplish anything. "How is this possible? I feel such a strong connection to you after only a matter of days." If he was on the fence about me, that would make him run miles away. I braced for his rejection.

"Thank God." He lowered his forehead to mine. "When you stopped talking to me, I was afraid my feelings were completely one-sided."

"You're relieved?" Most guys our age didn't want to hear girls talk about strong feelings. They wanted to be single and to mingle. "You aren't freaked out?"

"I was until you said that. The past two weeks have

been pure hell." He pulled back, and a huge smile spread across his face. "I feel the same thing, if not more, for you, and I understand that the intensity can be scary."

"Can be?" I still didn't understand how he wasn't freaking out. "That's why I stopped talking to you." Now that I'd started telling the truth, it was like my mouth had diarrhea. "This scares me. I didn't want to give you the opportunity to hurt me, and we can see how well that panned out. Even with distance my feelings for you grew, which makes no sense. Seeing you tonight, thinking you'd moved on ..." I couldn't finish that sentence.

"I'm so sorry." His head hung to the side. "I never meant to make you feel that way. It's the last thing I ever wanted to happen. You're the most important person in my life, and there is no one else who could ever capture my attention."

I believed him. I felt the exact same way. "But that's not normal to feel so strongly after such a short amount of time."

"In my family, it is." With his free hand, he curled his fingers into my hair. "When we find our person, we're all in."

"And that person is me?" The fact that his family commonly found someone they had these crazy feelings for was unbelievable.

"Yes." He stepped closer, his scent overloading my senses. "No one holds a candle to you."

Those words warmed the void inside me, and for the first time, my head didn't yell at me to stop. It had taken tonight for me to realize I needed him. I stood on my tiptoes and pressed my lips to his, wanting him to know I was done fighting. The jolt bolted between us, and my tongue licked across his mouth. Everything around us disappeared, and my focus was entirely on him.

A low growl emanated from his chest, throwing my

hormones into overdrive. He opened his mouth, and his tongue swept into mine. The vanilla taste was better than I remembered, and my head grew dizzy.

I slipped my hands under his thin sweater, enjoying the feel and warmth of his skin on mine. I'd never been so brazen before, but he was driving me mad.

His hands dropped to my waist and pulled me against him.

Then someone cleared her throat, tugging me back to the world around us.

CHAPTER THIRTEEN

I wanted to bury my face into Egan's massive chest and hide. I had an inkling it was Sadie who had caught us in our passionate embrace. I licked my lips, enjoying his lingering taste.

But I wouldn't cower, not this time. I pulled away slightly, but Egan's arm wrapped around my waist, anchoring me to him. He wanted me to stay close, and it thrilled me more than I'd ever admit.

"Is ... uh ..." Sadie grinned. "Is everything all right?"

"Really, babe?" Donovan chuckled and took her hand. "I'm thinking they're more than okay."

My face was on fire, so I changed the subject. "I'm sorry about earlier and the past few weeks. I've been rude to all of you, and it was uncalled for. I just got ..." I paused, searching for the best word.

"Overwhelmed?" Donovan threw out. "Unsteady? Scared?"

That brought my struggle to light. It hadn't been one thing but all three. "How did you know?"

He turned his focus on Sadie and took her hand. "Let's

just say you aren't the only one who's experienced something like this. It's a lot at first."

"You have a connection like this too?" I'd only read about stuff like this in books, and now I'd learned that another couple had this.

"Yes, we do." Sadie nodded. "It was a similar situation to you and Egan; I knew there was a chance to have a connection this strong with someone, and Donovan had no clue. We fought the connection at first too."

"She's right." Donovan scrunched his face. "I was a complete asshole."

"I wasn't much better." Sadie kissed his cheek. "But we've made it, and that's all that matters."

I completely understood that sentiment.

"Roxy and the others told us to meet them at the Student Center." Sadie lifted an eyebrow. "Do you two want to join us?"

"It's up to Jade," Egan said, his focus only on me.

My heart screamed no, but I'd been an ass to all of them. "Do you mind?"

"If that's what you want, then of course I don't." He pressed his lips to mine. "Whatever I can do to make you happy."

Okay, maybe I'd made the wrong call. We could be doing more of this instead, and honestly, I'd kind of prefer it.

Donovan laughed. "You better snatch her before she changes her mind."

"Leave them alone," Sadie chastised. "I'm thrilled for them."

There was no way I could've fought this any longer. Each day had chipped my will away. Even if I hadn't seen Amber all over him, I would've said screw it, just not nearly as fast. In a way, I was thankful she'd made me wake up sooner and put myself out of this misery.

"I need to do something about my raccoon eyes first." I gestured to the pronounced bags under my eyes.

"Oh, I can help with that." Sadie opened her purse and pulled out a makeup remover tissue. "Roxy makes me carry these around in case my makeup messes up. It does come in handy at times, but I'll never admit it."

Yeah, telling Roxy she was right would make her gloat for days. She and Lillith were forces to be reckoned with.

I pulled away from Egan, grabbed the cloth, and wiped under my eyes until no black rubbed off any longer. "Thanks."

Egan ran a finger along my chin. "Let's go. I'm starving."

"Didn't you eat already?" I had no clue how long I'd been in my car, but I figured it had been long enough for them to have eaten and come back to me wallowing in self-pity.

"Of course not." He moved so only one arm remained wrapped around me as he faced the Student Center. "When we realized you'd left, we were out of there in minutes."

That meant so damn much to me. "I hate that I ruined your night out."

"We didn't really want to eat there anyway." Donovan shivered. "Egan and I used to work there, and they weren't too happy about how we left, so we welcomed the excuse to get out of there."

"Then why go there in the first place?" That sounded like they'd been asking for punishment.

"We were looking for someone." Sadie tugged Donovan's hand and strolled toward the building, turning her back to us. "But they weren't there."

I quickly locked my car. Then Egan and I followed behind them. I asked, "Who was it?"

"I'm not sure of his name." Sadie glanced over her shoulder at me. "But we would know if we saw him."

That was vague and ominous, but I didn't want to push. They were already being super nice about me blowing them off for the past two weeks.

I was relieved that the Student Center wasn't super packed. Most people were hanging out off-campus and partying, being college students and all. That wasn't how I rolled. I liked being firmly in control, which was the opposite of what happened when alcohol was involved.

My eyes located their crew at the back of the room. Naida was the only one missing. Two tables were pushed together, making room for eight. Lillith and Katherine sat across from each other at the end. Axel and Roxy had their backs to us.

"Holy shit." Lillith rubbed her eyes and smirked. "Are my eyes playing tricks on me?" She looked at Roxy, who sat right across from her, and pointed at me.

I wasn't sure if I'd rather they give me a hard time or ignore me out of anger. I hated being the center of attention.

Roxy faced us and waggled her eyebrows. "I don't believe they are, and a certain huge guy has an arm wrapped protectively around her, so I'm thinking he finally locked her down."

"You two, stop." Katherine smacked Lillith on the arm. "Don't embarrass the poor girl."

"You're right." Lillith pouted. "She might disappear and hide for another couple of weeks."

I stood on my tiptoes and whispered in Egan's ear, "I'm never going to live this down, am I?"

"No." Axel rubbed Roxy's shoulder. "You aren't. Roxy

is as loyal as they come, but she'll throw out every wrong thing you've done to her any chance given."

How the hell had he heard me? I'd been quiet. "Do you have supersonic hearing?"

Egan tensed beside me.

"Phew. Please." Roxy rolled her eyes. "You aren't nearly as quiet as you think."

Apparently not. I squared my shoulders, needing to own up to how I'd treated everyone. "I just wanted to say I'm sorry about everything." I'd keep it vague since I had a feeling Roxy would drag it out as much as humanly possible.

Roxy tapped her finger on her lip as she pulled at the gold dress that hugged her body and complemented her complexion. "For what, exactly?"

"Roxy," Egan warned. "She's had a hard enough time. You should understand that."

"Fine." She placed her hand on the table and pursed her lips. "Take all my fun away."

"She should understand?" My attention went straight to Egan. "What do you mean?"

"They have a connection like ours." Egan's hand swallowed mine whole. He was huge, warm, and the kindest person I'd ever met. "They struggled at first too."

"Are you all family?" He'd said that his family knew connections like this existed. I hadn't considered that a group as close as them could be blood.

"I sure hope not." Roxy snorted. "Otherwise, we've been doing some pretty illegal stuff every night."

"Seriously?" Lillith groaned. "You guys were making sexual innuendos less than two minutes ago. I was hoping for a longer break."

"Stop the hate." Roxy pulled out the chair beside her

and patted it. "Come sit with me, Jade. We have plenty to catch up on."

"Do I have to?" I glanced at Sadie for help. "She's going to make me uncomfortable."

"It builds character." Roxy pointed at the seat. "Now get your ass over here so we can chat."

Sadie shrugged. "Sorry, but you'll have to fend for yourself on this one."

I deserved that. I walked over and plopped onto the seat next to her. My body tensed until Egan sat next to me and took my hand in his. Just his touch calmed me. I'd experienced the same thing the night I'd stumbled upon that dead girl.

"What's up?" I asked just as I inhaled the delicious scent of her hamburger. My stomach rumbled, and I realized how famished I was. I'd skipped dinner because I usually snacked throughout my shift, but now that I'd calmed down, I was starving.

Egan released my hand and stood. "Hey, I'll be right back." He kissed my cheek and headed toward the cafeteria.

"I'll join you." Donovan jumped to his feet and brushed his fingers on Sadie's arm. "I'll grab us something and be right back."

"Don't be long." Sadie blew him a kiss.

"Maybe I should go join them." Axel shook his head as he scanned the table full of women. "It was bad enough when it was three against one, but now we're talking about five."

"Oh, grow a pair," Roxy teased as she pushed his arm.

"No, but seriously." Lillith leaned over the table, her eyes more maroon than normal. "What's it like to kiss him?"

"What?" I knew women kissed and told, but I hadn't expected to be asked so blatantly. "Egan?"

"Have you been kissing someone else?" Roxy's eyes grew so wide they looked like they might pop out. "Who?"

"No one." This was bad. I didn't want Egan thinking I'd touched anyone else. I would never want to. "I'm just surprised you asked me that here."

"That either means it was remarkable or god-awful." Lillith leaned back in her seat and crossed her arms, causing her black long-sleeved shirt to wrinkle. "I'm hoping, for Egan's sake, that it's the remarkable one."

"Guys ..." Sadie giggled despite trying to maintain a solemn face. "Leave her alone."

Katherine leaned forward to see her around Lillith and said, "That isn't very convincing."

My mouth started running like every time I felt uncomfortable. "His lips are amazing. He tastes like the best part of a cinnamon roll—the vanilla frosting—and his tongue feels like velvet. When he touches me, it's like the world rights itself and I've finally found something I've desperately been missing without realizing."

"Velvet, eh?" Roxy chewed on her thumb. "I could see that."

"Really?" Axel's mouth dropped, and he stared at his girlfriend in disbelief. "I'm right here."

"You know you're it for me." She gestured to her neck. "There's no getting out of it, but Egan has always been a mystery and somewhat removed. To see the girl who turned him into a blubbering idiot and hear about that side of him has us all intrigued." She kissed Axel. "You have nothing to worry about."

"Damn straight, I don't," Axel growled and pulled her harder against his lips. "But you keep at it, and I'll have to kill him to make sure."

"Just kill her." I swore she and Lillith tried to embarrass

us every chance they got. It was like they liked the shock factor and fed off each other. "Problem solved for all parties."

"Hey." She jerked in my direction. "What the hell kind of traitor are you?" She smiled, clearly happy I was dishing it back.

Egan appeared, somehow balancing three trays. "Don't talk to her that way. I'd hate to have to drop all this food to come to her rescue."

"Don't worry. You wouldn't have to." I crossed my arms. "I can handle her on my own."

"And if you need help"—Lillith hit her chest and pointed at me—"I've got you."

"Man," Axel said, eyeing the three trays Egan placed on the table. "And here I thought you couldn't eat any more."

"Oh, stop." Egan put a tray in front of me that held chicken pasta, a cinnamon roll, and a Coke. "This one's for her."

I hadn't expected him to get me anything, but I couldn't say I was surprised. I'd planned on eating a peanut butter sandwich after getting settled, but this looked and smelled so much better. "Thank you, but you didn't have to."

"I know." He winked. "I wanted to."

For once, I believed him. He'd been trying to take care of me since the moment I'd seen him. Sadie and Donovan joined us, and we enjoyed our meal.

EGAN and I left the others and slowly headed back to the dorms. The entire evening had been fun, and I let myself relax and enjoy the company. We approached the girls' dorm, and I walked over to the brick wall, leaning against it.

A group of girls was hanging out in the lobby, and the last thing I wanted was for Egan to walk me upstairs and Vera to ask more questions. She was nice enough, but I wasn't ready for an interrogation.

He placed an arm on each side of me, trapping me.

If anyone else had done it, I would've freaked out, feeling claustrophobic, but not with him. It made me feel safe, and my body warmed at his close proximity.

"I had fun tonight." He looked deep into my eyes and sighed. "Having you there like that felt right."

"I know what you mean." I propped my head against the brick so I could see his handsome face. "Granted, it'd be nice if you and I could hang out alone sometime."

A large smile spread across his face, and his eyes appeared to glow faintly. "I am all for that, but I don't want to rush or pressure you."

"You're not." And that was one reason I trusted him completely. He knew what I needed. I placed my hands on his chest, enjoying the feel of his muscles. "And I'm all in."

"You have no idea how glad I am to hear you say that." He lowered his lips to mine but stopped a breath away. "I really would love to kiss you again."

"Then why wait?" I closed the distance between us, needing to reassure him. I was done letting fear rule me.

I focused on his lips and taste. Even after eating, he still tasted like warm vanilla. I moaned before I could stop myself. I'd normally be embarrassed, but I didn't give a damn. I didn't want to stop.

His arm slid down my body and wrapped around me, pulling me flush against him. The feel of his front pressed against mine made my body turn hot. I'd never felt this way before, and I realized why people did stupid things in the heat of a moment. My mind was foggy, and I wanted more.

When I licked his lips, he opened his mouth, allowing me in. He matched me stroke for stroke, and a low groan came from the back of his throat. My hands snaked up into his hair, and my mind focused on everywhere that he touched.

"Egan," Donovan said right next to us. "I hate to interrupt, but we need your help." His tone held an edge. Something was definitely wrong.

CHAPTER FOURTEEN

Egan pulled back from me slightly and looked at Donovan. His voice was low, raspy—sexy. "This can't wait?"

"No, man. Sorry." Donovan's gaze darted to me and back to Egan. "It's something we need help with now."

"Is everything okay?" Not too long ago, we'd all been hanging out and having fun. Their demeanor had completely changed. "Is there something I can do?"

Axel lifted a brow at Egan.

"Nah, you go in and get some rest." Egan kissed my forehead and smiled. "You've had a long night, and I'm hoping we can hang out tomorrow." Fear filled his eyes.

Him worrying that I might say no gutted me. I'd really done a number on him and wished I could take it all back. "Of course, but I don't mind helping."

"I know." He leaned down and kissed me once more. "But I'm sure it's nothing. I'll come by in the morning, and we can have breakfast together.

"Sounds perfect." I wanted to insist on going, but exhaustion overtook me. The night had been an emotional rollercoaster, and the bed called my name. I pulled my phone out of my pocket and unlocked it. "What's your number? I'll text you so you can let me know when you're heading my way."

He cupped my face and rattled it off. He then kissed my forehead, walked over to the door, and opened it for me. "I'll see you soon."

Donovan and Axel fidgeted, ready to get him and go. I was holding up whatever they needed to do.

I almost pushed, wanting to join them, but Egan had made it clear that he didn't want me involved. I guessed it was something guy-related.

"Be careful." I brushed my fingers along his chest as I walked by and entered the building.

He shut the door and stayed in place, watching me the entire way to the elevator. The guys talked to him as I stepped into the elevator. As the doors shut, Egan turned, and the group hurried off, but the doors slid shut before I could figure out which direction they'd rushed off in.

I regretted not forcing myself on them or following them to see what they were up to, but the elevator was already moving, and I doubted I could find them.

Oh well. It was probably for the best. I fired off a quick text, of **It's me**, so he'd have my number.

When I reached my floor, I walked slowly down the hall. It wasn't bubbling with people like usual. Most of the rooms were silent, indicating people were still out partying; the few people who'd stayed in had their televisions on loud.

I opened the door to my dorm room and was surprised to find that Vera wasn't inside. She always was at this time. Her normally tidy side of the room had an open bag on her bed with clothes thrown everywhere.

She must have been in a hurry. Strange. But I wouldn't

worry about it; I was going to enjoy the alone time I'd found. She almost always sat at her desk, pouring over books all the damn time. I didn't get it.

After putting on pajamas, I climbed into the bed, facing the door. Right as my eyes began to close, my phone vibrated on my desk. I picked it up to find a text message from Egan.

Good night. I can't wait to see you tomorrow. Be there to get you at 9.

The amount of happiness I felt from a stupid text was insane, but I was giddy as fuck over the fact he'd made it a point to tell me good night. I typed out my response: **Good night. I can't wait either. I'll be ready.**

I placed the phone back on the desk and fell asleep with a grin.

RED and blue lights flickered against the gray walls, waking me. I sat up and looked out my window, which overlooked the boys' dorm and the parking lot. Four police cars and an ambulance were pulled right up to the curb, all with their lights flashing.

Something bad had happened. Could it be another dead body? That surely couldn't be why Egan and his friends had run off. They wouldn't get involved with something like that on purpose ... would they?

The doubt alone made me stand and glance at Vera's bed. It was after one in the morning, and she was still gone. What if she'd gotten hurt? Maybe I should've gone looking for her instead of going to bed.

Not bothering to put on blue jeans, I stayed in my long

flannel pants and long-sleeved shirt. I grabbed my jacket and slipped my tennis shoes on, rushing to get down there. If I'd gone to sleep while my roommate was being tortured or worse, I might not ever get over that.

Racing out the door, I opted for the stairs. I flew down them, each step faster than the last. I reached the bottom of the stairs in half the time it normally took me. File that under "weird" and something to address at a later date.

Outside, two paramedics pushed a stretcher out from the walkway between Webster Hall and the library. A breeze blew the sheet off the person's face, and my eyes landed on familiar dark hair, a white button-down shirt, and black slacks. My stomach roiled.

Amber.

But, why? She didn't go to this school. She went to the local community college.

Egan and their entire group of friends stepped out from between the two buildings behind the paramedics.

Somehow, they'd known about this girl. And of course, the girls had been included, but not me.

"Jade," Egan called out. His eyes had taken on a glow. "Go back inside."

Really? He thought he could tell me what to do? That was not how this worked, and he'd be finding that out right now. I marched a few steps toward them, but Amber's neck caught my attention, stopping me in my tracks.

Her throat had been gouged over and over like something had repeatedly stabbed it or pecked at it. Blood congealed around the wound, but her eyes were frozen open, now a dark green color instead of the sparkling green I was used to seeing. Unable to look into them any longer, I focused back on her neck. The markings reminded me of the girl I'd found with her eyes gone. My stomach roiled again. How did this keep happening?

As the paramedics pushed her past me, I couldn't look away. Deep frowns marred the two men's faces, and their shoulders drooped. There was no helping her. Someone would have to call her parents and inform them that their child was dead.

Egan reached me and pulled me into his arms. "Jade."

"You knew." I pushed back from him and glared. My hands shook with anger. "That's why you ran off earlier."

"Look, I need you to go back inside." He opened the door and waved me in. "It's not safe out here."

He wasn't listening to me. He was too hell-bent on forcing me away. "But it isn't too dangerous for them?" I pointed at Sadie and the other girls. Even Naida was here. It burned. I'd let my guard down and thought I might actually be part of their group, but clearly, I wasn't. "Just not me. Why? I'm not part of your clique?" Something white-hot coursed through my body, burning me. Oddly, it didn't hurt. Rather, it was invigorating.

"No, that's not it." Egan lifted a hand. "We didn't … Just, please, go back inside."

"Egan," Sadie warned. "We need to go somewhere else."

"Like hell! You're not leaving me behind." They had to know more. Something deep in my gut told me that. "I want to know everything. What aren't you telling me?" They wouldn't push me away like a nobody any longer. If I let them discard me, they'd continue to do it.

"Honey—" Egan pleaded.

"She's either in or out," Naida said. "I told each of you that getting her involved was a mistake, but none of you listened. It's time to decide. Pick a side."

"Look at you," Roxy snickered. "Learning some slang. It's about damn time."

Ignoring Roxy, I asked Egan. "What is she talking about?" Out of all of them, I was surprised Naida wanted them to tell me everything, but he would be the one to tell me. If he believed in our connection, it was time for him to prove it.

"They're coming," Donovan whispered. "We need to at least pretend we aren't fighting."

I scanned, seeing no one, unsure what he meant until four police officers marched from the woods, coming into view. "How did you know that?" There was no way he could've known unless they weren't entirely human. But that was impossible. Those types of creatures didn't exist outside of stories.

"Please, stay calm," Katherine said with concern. "Naida's right, and if he won't tell you what's going on, I will."

That was enough for me.

The officers approached and stopped a few feet away.

The oldest one nodded, and the lines of his face deepened. "That's it for tonight. Give us a call if you remember anything else." He handed Egan a card. "And all of you need to go inside."

"Yes, sir," Egan replied. "Let us know if we can help out with anything too."

"You guys finding her was enough." The older officer hung his head. "I only wish we could've saved her."

"Us too," Sadie said with remorse.

The youngest officer grimaced. "With that kind of wound, it wouldn't have mattered."

"That's enough for tonight." The older one motioned to his men. "Let's get moving."

Donovan nodded. "We will do just that."

The officers headed to their patrol cars as we stood there, watching them go. There was no way in hell I would even pretend to go inside. If Egan had his way, he'd run off to keep me out of the loop. I stayed firmly in place and turned my full attention on him. "Spill."

"Not here." Egan scanned the area like he thought someone might overhear us. "We can talk tomorrow."

"No." I stood tall and lifted my chin. "I let my guard down with you. With all of you." I looked at each one of them, except Naida. "And I regret it."

"Don't say that." Egan grimaced and reached for my hand. "We're only trying to protect you."

I dodged him and clenched my teeth. "I am more than capable of protecting myself."

"You are *mine* to protect," Egan growled. His eyes glowed, and his pupils turned into slits. "There is nothing more important to me."

The first day here, I'd thought I'd imagined his pupils doing that. Fear rocked through me, and I blinked, thinking my mind was seeing things. But they stayed the same.

"Egan, you need to calm down." Sadie grabbed my arm and pulled me toward her. "You're getting too wound up."

"Do not touch her!" he roared and pushed Sadie off me. "No one but I can."

"Hey now." Donovan sprang into action and shoved Egan hard. "Calm down."

I stood there in shock at what he'd done. He'd always been caring and sweet, but he'd just pushed his best friend.

Sadie didn't seem angry, though. She placed a hand on Donovan, and as soon as she touched him, he calmed down. I'd never seen anything like it before.

Egan took a few menacing steps toward Donovan, ready to fight. He fisted his hands, prepared to punch him.

"You need to make him focus on you," Roxy said, pointing at Egan. "Or they're going to fight, and it'll cause a huge problem."

A little more direction would've been nice, but instinct took over. I stepped between Donovan and Egan, effectively shutting Egan down.

I clutched both of his fists. "Calm down. They aren't doing anything. You're acting irrationally."

"You do realize telling an irrational person that they're being irrational isn't the smartest move," Lillith scoffed. "I know it pisses me off more."

"That's because you're female," Axel retorted.

"Oh, hell no," Roxy gasped and smacked him on the back of the head. "That's not cool."

None of them were normal. I hadn't noticed how much until this moment. Who cracked jokes when two friends were about to beat each other down?

Egan's breathing calmed, but his pupils remained slitted.

Even though part of me was freaked out, an equally large part wasn't fazed by his odd-shaped eyes. "Please, tell me everything," I said, soft and non-threatening.

"Okay." He sighed and glanced around the group. "But not here. It's late, and we all need to get our rest."

"If this is your way of getting out of it—"

"It's not." He ran a hand through his hair. "I promise. But we just found Amber dead, and you're in your pajamas."

When he laid it out like that, I couldn't argue. Damn him and his logic. "Then, first thing in the morning." I wouldn't let him get out of it completely. They were holding back something huge, and not knowing was driving me insane.

His face fell. "But I kind of wanted to enjoy some time with you."

"No, you obviously have secrets." I gestured to the library and to Naida. Not to mention his eyes doing freaky shit. "I'm not going anywhere with you until I know what you're hiding. I opened up to you, and you're refusing to do the same?"

"It's just—"

"Let me make it clear." I placed my hands on my hips. "Don't bother coming tomorrow if you aren't going to tell me everything." His hesitation about telling me what it was threw up giant red flags. I'd let my guard down too soon, but I wouldn't be treated like I wasn't an equal. I'd rather be alone.

I turned on my heel and walked into the dorm, letting the door slam shut behind me. I left a part of my heart behind, but I forced my feet forward.

The door opened behind me, and he called out, "Wait."

CHAPTER FIFTEEN

Everything inside me demanded I stop, but he was playing a game I didn't like. Somehow, I continued my march to the elevator. If I caved, it would set a precedent I wasn't okay with.

"Wait." Egan's footsteps grew closer as he rushed to catch up. "I'll tell you." His voice sounded broken.

I stopped and turned, facing the empty lobby. "When?" I was tired of bending to the will of everyone around me—my mom, Sarah, and now Egan. Committing to a time would push this along.

Childhood memories flashed in my mind. The times Sarah would punch me for being five minutes late from school. When Mom would purposely turn a blind eye to the abuse. The near-constant insults about being worthless and an annoyance. Telling me daily since I was eight that I would never amount to anything and I was lucky to have a bed because I didn't even deserve that.

I was done being the victim and letting others make the rules. That had been the point of running away to Kortright.

Not being with him would hurt like hell, but it would be worse to lose myself.

"It's late." He scratched the back of his neck. "And you really need your rest, so you should sleep in tomorrow. We can put off our morning like initially planned."

He offered to tell me everything, and then in the next breath, he tried to push off the conversation. "Whatever." I shouldn't have been surprised. I gestured to his friends, watching outside the door. "Go back to them. There's nothing left to say. You know how to get a hold of me when you're ready."

It hurt so damn much that he was keeping things from me, but I couldn't change that. I inhaled sharply like the air around me could strengthen my resolve, pivoted toward the elevator, and pushed the up button.

He exhaled loudly. "Okay, let's talk now. You're right. You have a right to know." He sounded gutted. "But we need to go somewhere private to talk."

His words validated my fear. It had to be bad. "My roommate isn't here." Under normal circumstances, being alone in a room with him would be a bad idea, but that wasn't a problem tonight. He couldn't distract me from what I wanted to know, and if things went south, I was surrounded by girls who'd hear my screams.

"Of course she's not." He laughed without humor. "Well, okay then."

My nerves frayed even more. There was no reason I should be feeling trepidation. The elevator doors slid open, and Egan waved to his friends before getting in.

I had to keep reminding myself they were his friends. They were almost a family, one I wasn't part of even if I felt like I had a connection with them.

Time crawled the entire way to the room. Now that I knew answers were imminent, I was equally thrilled and terrified. I might finally understand the connection between us.

I steadied my hands, opened the door to my room, and waved him inside. "Come on in."

He hesitated then sighed and entered the room. "Do you know when she's coming back?" His focus settled on the Star Wars poster on her side of the room.

"No, but I don't think it'll be tonight." We really didn't keep each other abreast of our schedules. I only let her know when I worked so she wouldn't be scared when I got in late. "She's never been gone like this, so she probably went back home. She's not a social butterfly."

A frown marred his face as I sat on my bed.

I placed my hands in my lap and arched an eyebrow. "So get on with it."

"Once you learn everything, there is no going back," he said ominously.

"I don't care," I said, my voice cracking. Surely, this didn't have anything to do with the girls' deaths. I'd found the first girl, and they hadn't been anywhere around. I'd left them in the Student Center. "I want to know, or you need to go."

"All right." He ran his hands through his hair, mussing it up. "This will sound crazy, but I need you to keep an open mind."

"That's not surprising." There was something different about their group. I'd felt it on day one, but the more time I spent around them, the more things I noticed. "What are you, spies?"

He barked out a laugh, but his eyes were devoid of humor, making me even more uncomfortable.

"I wish that was it." He paced between the beds. "My friends and I are different."

"Tell me something I don't know," I snapped, my patience wearing thin. "But how are you different?"

"You really are like Sadie." He rubbed his temples. "You just cut through all the bullshit. That's one of the things I like about you."

The comparison to Sadie rubbed me the wrong way. "Are you saying you're into Sadie too?"

"What?" His mouth dropped open, and he blinked. "No. Not at all. You're it for me. It's just a similar trait that I find endearing."

I wanted to push it, but I had to keep my jealousy at bay. There were more important factors at hand. "Can we stop talking about *her* and get to the point?"

"Jade." He stared deep into my eyes. "There is absolutely nothing to worry about. Sadie and I are just friends. Nothing more. We were never anything more. You don't need to feel threatened. I was stupid to compliment you like that, and I'm sorry. I keep messing up."

"Why shouldn't I feel threatened?" Sadie was like the perfect person. "She's gorgeous, kind, and there's something about her that puts me at ease."

"But she's not my mate." He sucked in a breath. "You are."

"Of course I'm not all those things." Tears stung my eyes. "So that's what we are? Friends?"

"Dammit." He dropped my hand and pulled at his hair. "I'm doing this all wrong. You're more than that. You're sexy, infuriating, and so damn strong. When you smile, it's like everything in the world gets righted. You're becoming the oxygen I need to breathe." He cupped his hands around mine.

"But you just said we're mates." I didn't think he'd be so cruel to mess with me like this. He'd say we were friends in one breath; then in the next, he'd give my heart hope. All of these confusing emotions were driving me insane.

"Mates as in fated mates. Some call them soulmates," he said as he angled his body toward me. "That's what I'm trying to say. We are two halves of one soul, and we found each other."

"Fated mates?" I tried to scoot farther back, but my traitorous body wouldn't do it. I needed to be near him. "Those aren't real." Those were my favorite type of romance stories to read, but that's what they were. Stories.

"They are in my world." He winced. "In *our* world."

"What the hell does that mean?" My voice rose in anger and frustration. "Just tell me." My mind was racing at all the possibilities, but each one was impossible ... wasn't real.

"My group of friends and I aren't human." He rubbed his hands together. "We're supernaturals."

"Egan, stop fucking with me." He had to be messing with me, but the explanation made sense. How Egan had heard the scream that night when he'd been back in the Student Center. How his eyes turned to slits. And how they could hear me when I whispered. But that was insane.

"I'm not." He rubbed his finger along the top of my hand gently. "I know it sounds crazy, but that's why you feel the connection between us the way you do."

"So what are you?" My mind was running so fast I couldn't even process my thoughts. "Vampires?" Of course, *Twilight* was the only thing I landed on.

"Katherine and Lillith are."

Their all-liquid diet made all kinds of sense now. "Are you serious?" I touched my neck as a chill ran down my spine.

"Yes, but they don't drink straight from humans, and they don't kill." He tightened his hold on my hand. "You are completely safe. If they were a threat, I wouldn't let them near you."

"So what is everyone else, then?" I was struggling to remain calm. I pulled my hands from his.

"Donovan, Axel, and Roxy are wolf shifters." He watched my reaction and flinched. "Naida is a fae. Sadie is a hybrid of fae and wolf shifter. And I'm ..." He trailed off.

For him to act like that made me even more nervous. "You're what?"

He stared at me looking for something. "A dragon shifter."

"A dragon?" His eyes turning to slits made sense now, but they were huge and scary. "You've got to be kidding me." I had to be dreaming. I was sure this was just a nightmare. I chuckled, and he frowned.

Hurt turned his eyes almost black. "Look, I know it's a lot to take in." He raised his hands and dropped them into his lap. "But if you think about it—"

"I don't want to think about it." This was all too damn much. A bird or some other animal had killed Amber tonight, and I'd just learned that supernaturals were real. "This is insane. You're telling me that everything I've read or watched on television is real?"

"Most parts are." He rubbed a hand down his chin. "Usually, stories are based on real things. It's just that supernaturals don't want humans to know about our existence. It would cause mass hysteria."

"Then why are you telling me this?" I stood and backed against the wall, needing distance from him. If he was a dragon, he could hurt me without trying. "That defeats the purpose of keeping it a secret."

"Because you're my mate, Jade. Those rules don't apply to you." He took a step toward me. "You're different. You and I are meant to be together, meaning you're now part of this world."

His fingertips brushed my cheek again, and I felt so safe despite everything I'd learned. I inadvertently stepped into him, drawn to him, proving our bond was extraordinary.

"Please don't." I pushed his hand down, not wanting him close. Every time he touched me, my mind turned fuzzy, and I needed a clear head. "What you're telling me is crazy." Hurting him was the last thing I wanted to do, but this was too much.

He flinched and dropped his hand to his side. "I can only imagine." Concern etched into his forehead. "I don't want to throw you into a world you want no part of."

"Yet you did." He'd taken care of me because he felt like he had to, and he'd kissed me while knowing about our connection. His actions felt like a betrayal. "You should have told me straight away." By not doing so, he'd allowed our connection to grow. Unshed tears burned my eyes. I'd trusted him completely. "Instead of manipulating me."

"I didn't manipulate you." His shoulders sagged, and he closed his eyes. "I was scared to tell you. You're too important to me, and the thought of losing you petrified me."

"You're right. Manipulation isn't the right word, but you lied to me." Hurt coursed through me, and the cold spot inside my chest felt like a weight, adding to my pain. Not only had he not told me, but none of the others had either, cutting me deeper. "I thought I was going crazy. I didn't understand what was going on, and you let me struggle. I'm human, and I've never felt even half of what I feel for you for someone else before. The connection is so strong it takes my breath away at times."

He hung his head and brushed a tear off my cheek. The jolt between us came to life. Our bond had already gotten stronger tonight.

"You're right. I did." He closed his eyes and shook his head. "I'm so sorry. I never meant to do that to you, but the urge to be close to you was overwhelming. I needed to be near you. When we're apart, it's like a piece of me is gone."

"Maybe you didn't mean to hurt me, but you did. I should've known before we kissed tonight. You should've told me everything." I shuddered and rubbed my hands along my arms as cold settled in my bones, adding regret to my emotions. I needed to sort through everything. If he stayed, I'd say things I would regret. "I'm sorry, but you need to go." Saying the words physically hurt me. I didn't want him to leave, but him staying would only result in us hurting each other.

"What?" His head snapped up, and his eyes darkened to a rustic gold. "No."

"Yes, you do." Something brushed against my skin, urging me to hold him, but I pushed it away. I didn't need to make any decisions right now. "I need time alone to process."

"Can I come back in the morning?" He sounded like a little boy.

"I'm not sure." I picked up my phone. "I'll text you when I'm ready."

"Jade." He reached for me.

"Stop." If he touched me, I'd crumble into mush. "Please, just go."

His eyes glistened as he ran his hands through his hair. Somehow, he looked only about half of his normal height. He rasped, pain clear in his tone, "We always come back to here." He stepped toward the door. "At first, you asked me to 'Please give you space.' Now it's, 'Please just go.' You're always pushing me away."

"That's the thing." I glared at him. I wasn't sure if he was trying to make me feel guilty. "It's not about pushing you away. It's about processing everything in my own time."

"Okay." He opened the door and paused. He turned toward me. "This time, I'll give you all the space you need." His breath caught as he glanced at me, looking so broken. Then he walked out the door, and when the door shut behind him, I crumpled to the floor.

I woke up with a pounding headache. This had to be what a hangover felt like. In all fairness, I had one—an emotional hangover. I'd stayed up till four, crying like a newborn baby. If I'd thought the episode in my car was bad, I'd been wrong —so damn wrong.

My eyes were tender, so I grabbed my phone and turned on the camera immediately regretting it. My reflection staring back at me was one of horror. My hair had knots in it, and my eyes were almost swollen shut. The slits I could see were dark red. I looked like I'd been ridden hard or gotten the flu.

There was no way I could make it into work today. I snatched the phone off the desk and felt a little disappointed when I didn't have a message from Egan. But I had to remember, I'd asked for this.

Quickly texting Ollie to inform him I felt worse than yesterday, I tossed the phone on the bed and flopped back onto my pillow. I had no energy to get out of bed.

The shock of Egan's revelations last night still hadn't fully processed. That his friends were various kinds of supernaturals was insane. The fact I believed him made me certifiable.

Each one of them was so genuine and embraced who they were, unlike anyone else I'd ever met before. Maybe that was the missing piece that made it all click together. They were confident in themselves in a way no human could ever be.

Growing up, I'd been petrified of the dark, so to have my childhood terrors come to life and be real unsettled me. Had I somehow known as a child that the supernatural stories were real since I was a dragon's destined mate? It sounded crazy, but right then, that was my norm.

Egan's handsome face appeared in my mind, and just seeing it brought a sense of calm over me. Surely, if he were a real threat, I'd be naturally inclined to fear him, not tugged toward him. But could I knowingly enter into a life that was so hard to accept?

I didn't understand what being part of that life meant. I had a feeling it was completely different from what I'd ever known.

At the same time, the thought of not being with Egan was too painful to consider. But what would I have to give up to be with him?

Whichever decision I made would require a sacrifice.

On Monday morning, I stepped out of the dorm room. The entire weekend, I hadn't left except to run to the bathroom. Vera had never returned from wherever the hell she'd gone, so I was able to eat and drink in the room.

Egan had left me alone as he'd promised. I'd expected a few calls or texts, but it was radio silence.

That worked, though, since I'd been in hiding. I'd finally come to a decision, one I wasn't sure about. But when had anything ever truly gone my way?

It was early as hell, but I couldn't sleep and needed to do this. With shaky hands, I pulled up Egan's name and sent him a message. **Hey, can you come outside so we can talk?**

My heart pounded against my ribcage. That was how nervous I was. Then my phone buzzed. **On my way.**

CHAPTER SIXTEEN

Waiting for him outside the dorm was probably the hardest thing I'd ever done. I didn't know what to expect, and the fact that I would be solidifying my decision churned my stomach. He must have been going through the same thing this past month while being around me.

The sky was still pitch dark, and the cold was penetrating without the sun to warm the air. I tapped my fingers on my jeans. I wore a thicker black sweater and jacket since it was below freezing. Every breath puffed out in a cloud.

The campus was still asleep, and no one was around since it was before six in the morning.

Footsteps came from behind, startling me. I spun around, ready to defend myself, and found Egan walking toward me.

"Couldn't sleep?" I'd been worried about waking him up, but obviously, I shouldn't have been.

"No." Dark circles lined his eyes, and his hair was in complete disarray. He wore his usual jeans and a thin sweater, but they were wrinkled. I was pretty sure it was the exact outfit he'd worn the last time I saw him.

"Are you out here alone?" I hated the thought of something happening to him.

He stopped several feet away like he didn't want to come closer. "Yeah, keeping an eye out for anything strange."

It burned. Maybe he'd decided he didn't want me. Like he'd said, I'd been difficult this entire time. Maybe my last breakdown had been his tipping point. I kept pushing him away. "With all these deaths, you shouldn't risk it."

"Would you care if something did happen?" His expression was unreadable as he watched for my reaction.

His question stung, but I deserved it. "Of course I would." I couldn't survive him not being alive. "That's why I need you to stay safe."

"You have a funny way of showing it." He crossed his arms, unapproachability radiating off him.

"If you aren't up for talking, we can meet up later." I cleared my throat. "Or not at all." With the vibe rolling off him, he might not be interested in talking to me ever again.

He lifted an eyebrow, and his nose wrinkled. "Is that your way of telling me your decision?"

That was when it hit me—he expected me to end things with him. "No, it's not, but you look like you can barely stand. Have you slept?"

"It's hard to sleep when the one person who holds my heart wants nothing to do with me." He lifted his hands in front of him. "Please, just tell me what you want instead of dragging this out."

"First, I have a few questions." I didn't know how any of this worked.

"You'll be safe." His eyes glowed. "I'll make sure of it. You can pretend that the supernatural world doesn't exist. You can pretend I don't exist."

He looked like a heartbroken man. He only needed me to confirm what he expected. "That's going to be hard to do."

"I can leave if you want me to." He put his hands into his pockets. "I can be gone in a few hours if that's what you need."

"But I don't want you to leave," I whispered, knowing he could hear the words.

He stilled, and he blinked. "What are you saying?"

The cold spot in my chest warmed as I watched his face change from broken to hopeful. The warmth had to be linked to him. That would've sounded insane two days ago, but not anymore. I had so much to learn.

My heart raced as I moved closer to him, but I stopped a few inches away, not confident enough to bridge the entire distance. "I'm sorry about everything, but you've got to understand that my life hasn't been the easiest. I ran away to come here."

"What do you mean you 'ran away'?"

"My dad died when I was younger, and Mom almost didn't survive it." I'd never talked about this with anyone. It hurt too much. "She couldn't hold a job because she could barely function. So we went to live with her sister." That was when my bad dream had turned into a nightmare. "My aunt hates me, and she's made my life a living hell. I was supposed to go to a local college fall semester, and she threw a fit, so when I got accepted here, I ran. Neither one of them knows where I am."

"I'm so sorry." He scratched at his longer-than-usual stubble. "I had no clue."

"No, don't." I hated when people apologized for things they had no control over. "But you need to understand that I came here to figure out who I am and what I want to become. I swore I'd never allow a man to have that much control over my happiness like Dad had over Mom."

He frowned and nodded. "I understand that. So meeting me has been very problematic and horrible timing."

"The worst timing." I touched his arm, and the jolt crashed into me. "But I wouldn't change it for anything."

He sucked in a breath, and his eyes flicked to mine. "What do you mean?"

"Thank you for not giving up on me." I licked my lips, still unsure. "I'm all in if you still want me."

His strong arms wrapped around me, pulling me tight against his chest. "I'll always want you. Even if you decide you don't want to be with me, I'll never get over you."

"I couldn't get over you either." I pulled back and stared at him. "And I don't want to try." Our connection came to light, and I stood on my tiptoes as his mouth pressed against mine.

I had so many questions, but we deserved to have this moment. I opened my mouth, inviting his tongue inside. His sweet vanilla taste overwhelmed me in the best way possible. A shiver coursed through my body as his scent and taste surrounded me.

He leaned back, his eyes light gold. "Let's get you inside. It's freezing out here."

"My roommate is still gone," I offered. "Why don't we go up there?"

"Okay." He nodded and took my hand, and we headed inside.

In my dorm room, I stood between the beds and faced him, feeling awkward. I was very inexperienced when it came to guys.

"You don't need to be nervous." He took my hand and pulled me onto the bed beside him. "There are some things we still need to talk about, and I would never want to do anything that made you feel uncomfortable."

"There's more to tell?" The last bit of news had been a doozy, so I hadn't expected there to be any more.

"Yeah, you freaked out and didn't give me a chance to tell you everything." He played with my fingers. "But before you get in too deep, I need to tell you all of it."

"Shoot." I scooted closer to him. I was pretty sure nothing could scare me off. "What else is there?"

He swallowed, his doubt resurfacing. "The more we connect, and especially when we complete the bond, our souls will connect."

That didn't sound as bad as he was making it. "I think I'm still missing something."

"Essentially, you'll slowly change into a dragon shifter like myself." He patted his chest. "You'll become a supernatural."

All right, I'd spoke too soon. "How is that possible?"

"The connection causes us to become one, in a way." He avoided my gaze completely. "And since I'm already part shifter and human, I won't change. But since you are fully human, you'll be impacted the most."

"Can I control it?" I knew so little. "Will it hurt?"

"Wait ..." A huge smile crossed his face. "You don't need to think about this again?"

"No." Being with him felt right, and even considering the alternative ripped my heart wide open. "This past weekend put things into perspective. I was afraid our connection would make me weak, but being without you felt like I wasn't whole. Why would I put us through that when we could be so much happier together?"

"You have no clue how scared I was." He rested his forehead against mine and ran his fingers through my hair. "Thinking of a life without you in it ..."

"Hey, it's okay." I kissed him gently. "I'm not going anywhere. But will it hurt?"

"Mom said it didn't." He shook his head. "It's strange, but it didn't hurt her."

"Wait, your mom was human too?" I hadn't expected that.

He booped me on the nose. "A little secret that only dragon shifters know. All mates are human in the beginning."

"Others have gone through the same thing?" That was strangely comforting. At least, I wasn't odd or going against the grain. Maybe his people would be more accepting of me that way.

"Yes, granted I'm the first dragon who's found their mate in decades."

"Why is that?" This whole new world fascinated me.

"Because we were hunted." He paused. "We had to hide, but then we couldn't reproduce, so our kind started dying off. We can only reproduce with our fated mates. We had to do something, so that's one reason I'm here."

"To find mates?" Now he was telling me he was a matchmaker.

He laughed hard. The sound was breathtaking. I'd never heard him so happy before.

"No, that would be a disaster." He cupped my cheek. "But learning how to coexist with other supernaturals and humans again. That way, I can help the others adapt better and more strategically so they'll have a better chance at finding their mates."

"What if they can't find their mates?"

"Why did you come here?" He ran his fingertips down my arm. "Why Kortright?"

"I don't know." The day I stumbled upon the ad flitted through my mind. "I saw the campus and knew I needed to be here."

"The bond pulled you here just like it drew me here too. That's how dragons find their mates."

That sounded beautiful. "We were destined to find each other?"

"Yes, but boy, did I think we wouldn't get here," he said and kissed me.

My brain short-circuited at the feel of his lips and the pleasant jolt running through my body. I wanted to lose myself in all things Egan.

I pushed my hands into his hair and pulled him closer to me. I craved his touch. He eagerly returned each kiss and stroke of my tongue. A hand slipped under his sweater and my fingers traced his six-pack.

He groaned, "You'll be the death of me."

His words empowered me. I placed a hand on the back of his neck and slowly lay back on my bed. He crawled over me and placed his arms on either side. Feeling trapped had never excited me before.

Both hands slipped under his sweater and I tugged the hem toward his head.

He paused and pulled away. "We don't have to rush things."

"We've waited long enough." My body burned for him, literally. "Unless you don't want to." Doubt crept in.

"You have no idea how bad I want to." His pupils turned to slits. "But I don't want to scare you away again. This will really kick in the bond. Having sex pretty much completes it, except for the formal mating ritual done in front of our thunder."

"Thunder?" The way he looked at me nearly had me purring.

"That's what a group of dragons is called," he breathed.

My hands trembled as I unbuttoned his jeans. "You won't scare me. I need you."

"But you're shaking." His breath hit my face. "I don't want to pressure you."

"It's just that I'm a virgin." I closed my eyes, completely embarrassed. "I'm nervous, but there is no doubt in my mind."

"Hey." He pulled his sweater off and discarded it. "I am too. There is no reason to be nervous or embarrassed." He kissed my cheek and peppered kisses down my neck.

"Really?" I'd figured he'd been with a ton of women. He was sexy as hell. I noticed how many girls watched him. "You're a virgin too?"

"Yes. I never wanted anyone until you." He straightened to look into my eyes. "I figured there was no reason to have sex until I'd found my mate."

I'd been such an idiot for pushing him away. He was an old soul and a genuinely good person. His actions and thoughts proved just how rare of a treasure he was. I raised my lips to his. "Make love to me." I pulled my sweater off and tossed it on the ground.

A low growl emanated from him as he lowered himself on top of me. His hand snaked around my back to unfasten my bra. In seconds, I felt it unlatch, and he helped remove it from my arms.

"You're so beautiful." He captured my nipple in his mouth and sucked then nipped. A hand grazed down my stomach toward my pants.

New emotions flowed through me. His tongue flicked, and my entire body warmed even more. A deep ache inside caught me off guard.

His mouth worked magic on me as he unfastened my jeans. Words left me as I lifted my butt. He pushed down my jeans and panties, kissing down my stomach. My skin tingled where his mouth devoured me.

He stood and discarded the rest of his clothes then grabbed my pants and underwear, discarding them as well.

My eyes devoured every inch of him. His sun-kissed body deserved to be licked, and that day I'd seen the outline of him had grossly downplayed what he had to offer.

His eyes glowed as he dropped to his knees, placing his fingers on my core, and devoured my breast once more. He rubbed in circular motions, and white flames burned across my skin again. He slid his hand back, using his fingers to enter me. The intense sensation made my breath hitch.

My head rolled back, and I closed my eyes, overcome by emotions. I wrapped my fingers in his hair, pulling it hard, needing to release the tension. The friction increased as his hands did magical things to my body. If they could do this, anticipation thrummed through me over what came next. "Now. Please."

He removed his hand and situated himself between my legs. His tip touched right outside of me. He growled, "Let me know if it hurts." He propped himself on his elbows and kissed me.

I ran my hands down his back, his hard body primed and ready.

I bucked against him as he slowly entered me. Everything I'd heard said the first time hurt, but he thrust slowly and gently, each time only getting a little deeper than the last. My whole body jolted from our connection, and the cold spot warmed to piping hot, matching the intensity.

He groaned as he picked up the pace, slamming into me harder. "God, you feel good," he rasped as he kissed me again.

I dug my nails into his back as he slammed into me, making my insides shudder. I moaned and matched his pace, wanting him deeper.

I pushed him off me and onto his back. He was trying to take it easy, but something clawed inside me. I straddled him and slipped him inside me once more. He filled me even more, hitting exactly where I needed. I moved, pounding him inside me.

He groaned as his fingers grabbed my waist and bucked in rhythm.

Using the wall to steady myself, I felt my body tighten as something shifted inside me. I convulsed as an orgasm rocked my body, and Egan shook underneath me. We released at the same time, and something snapped between us. My vision went black.

CHAPTER SEVENTEEN

My eyes wouldn't open, and Egan's hands clutched my arms.

"Jade," he said with worry. "Jade." He gently rolled me off him and faced me. "Baby." His fingers touched my face as he turned me toward him.

I wanted to comfort him, but I didn't have control of my body. The white-hot flame surged inside me. It traveled to my center and poured into the cold spot. As the two conflicting emotions clashed, my body shivered.

"Dammit," Egan growled, grabbed the covers, and tucked them all around me.

But they didn't do any good. The two temperatures battled each other. More and more flames poured inside, filling the void like a glass, but it was a slow build. My heart raced, and my head pounded in sync.

My breathing became shallow, but my mind grew clearer. My thoughts processed faster than ever before.

As the flames filled the cup, energy exploded inside me. My skin tingled, and even my hair changed.

This had to be because we'd completed the bond. I could feel it taking hold.

"What did I do to you?" His words broke as he shook my shoulders. "Jade, wake up. Please."

Not being able to speak was a good thing just then. I'd have had a smart-ass reply. Being paralyzed was not high up on my list of things I wanted—I'd rather be awake and talking too—but that wasn't an option.

My heart rate increased as the magic took hold. My body grew stronger, and my hearing heightened. I could hear Egan's heartbeat and his lungs filling and contracting. A group of girls walked outside the dorm, talking about their weekend and how hungover they were. A bird chirped from miles away.

Egan moved away for a second, and I heard him messing with his phone. A ring on the other end pierced my ears. Right when I thought the voicemail would answer, a male's voice answered instead, "Hey, son."

"Dad, there's something wrong with Jade," Egan rasped. "She's not responding to me. I don't know what to do."

"What happened?" Concern laced Egan's dad's voice. "Is she hurt?"

"I ... I don't know."

His dad asked loudly, "How the hell do you not know if she's hurt? You can sniff out her wounds."

"She wasn't attacked. She's not hurt like that." Egan cleared his throat. "We solidified our bond, and right afterward, she crumpled against me."

If my body could move, I'd be hiding. He'd just informed his dad that we had sex and I'd passed out. I'd never even met the guy, and he already knew way too much about me. That would make meeting his parents very uncomfortable.

"Oh, son." His dad sighed. "You should've called me first so you and she were prepared."

"I did not want to have that conversation with you. Besides, it just kind of ..." Egan trailed off, searching for the right word. "... happened."

"After the huge fight you had, I guess I should've expected it. But since you two went from spending barely any time together to completing the bond, she's going through her change faster."

"What do you mean?" Egan turned back to me. "You never told me there was a fast-track option."

"When two people fight it like you two did, fate intervenes. Fate knows what she's doing, and she'll ensure you complete the bond sooner rather than later." His dad chuckled. "I should've warned you, but I didn't think about it. It's been a while since anyone's gone through this, but since she was so resistant, your bond kicked in harder. She'll be fine."

With everything going on inside me, his explanation made perfect sense. The tingling was already dulling, and I felt like a stronger version of myself just lying there.

"Okay." Egan sounded relieved. "Does it hurt when they transform?"

"From what your mother said, it didn't hurt one bit. She explained it more as feeling invigorating and different. The adjustment to her dragon will be harder, though, since the change wasn't as gradual and was basically sprung on her. Just be calm and call me later. Remember, she was born with her soul knowing this would happen one day, so her body is prepared to embrace it."

I hadn't thought about what becoming a supernatural really meant, but the fact that my body had known this would happen one day resonated with me. Well, okay, that was a stretch. But after the last few days, very little didn't make at least some sense to me. My entire world had changed in the blink of an eye.

"I can't lose her," Egan replied dejectedly. "We were finally making things right. If I lose her now—"

"Son, stop. You aren't going to. She'll be alert in a few minutes. Call me in ten if she hasn't woken, and I'll be there as fast as possible."

His father's concern warmed me. That was what parents should give their child. No wonder Egan had grown into such an amazing man.

"Thanks, Dad." Egan touched my arm. "I'll let you know either way. Love you." He dropped the phone and kissed my cheek. "I'm so sorry. I didn't know this would happen. Had I known, I would've been stronger and made us wait so things would be easier on you."

The tension in my body lessened, and my eyes opened. My breath hitched. I'd never seen things so clearly before. I could easily read the books on the other side of the room, whereas their spines would normally be a blur. And the sunlight shining through my window seemed brighter. I turned my head to him. "Hey," I said, my voice breaking.

"Oh, thank God." His forehead touched mine, and he kissed my cheek. "Are you okay?"

"Yeah, I think so." I smiled at him and slowly sat up. I glanced around the room, and my head swam. "Just feel a little strange." I steadied myself with an arm as I wobbled.

"Did it hurt?" he asked, sitting up next to me. The covers fell from his chest, giving me an amazing view of his muscles, each one defined and lickable.

My body warmed at the sight. Something inside me snapped. "No. Not at all." I kissed him hungrily, wanting him again already.

He growled and pulled me close to him. This was

different from before—more animalistic. He wasn't being gentle and was treating me more like an equal.

I reached down and took hold of him, need filling me again. His normal citrus smell turned spicy, and something inside me clawed more desperately than before. God, I didn't think it would be possible for him to smell even better.

His hands slipped between my legs again, but when he touched me, it felt more amazing—like I could feel more. His emotions slammed into mine, startling me. He felt so much for me that it almost took my breath away. We were completely smitten with each other.

You're so gorgeous. His words popped inside my mind. *And you're driving me insane.*

Startled, I pulled back. "What the hell just happened? You spoke inside my brain." Was I officially losing it?

"It's our mate bond." He grinned and rubbed my lip with his thumb. "Now that we've pretty much completed the bond, we can speak to each other through our minds, no matter the distance." He sucked on my bottom lip, and I gasped.

"Can you do that with others?" I wasn't sure how I felt about people being inside my brain. "Can you hear all my thoughts?"

"We can only do this with our mates. And your mind is projecting your thoughts at me. You'll have to learn how to block them and only let the ones you want me to hear trickle out." His fingers rubbed circles again. "I'm sure I'll also struggle since it's new for me too. Your dragon is calling out to mine."

"My dragon?" That had to be what I felt inside me. "You can sense her?"

"Yes. Can you not sense mine?"

Now that he'd mentioned it, maybe I could. There was such a strong connection between us now. "I think I can." I touched his chest, and both his skin and magic poured into me. It wasn't a jolt anymore but an exchange of power. The fact that we both needed to figure out our connection calmed me. I wasn't alone concerning everything.

He grabbed my waist and pulled me down, and I fell flat on the bed again. His lips were on my neck, and his teeth raked against my skin. He climbed on top of me, his fingers not missing a beat. My body spasmed as pleasure coursed through me.

I moved my hand, wanting to please him too. His lips landed on mine as a finger flicked my nipple.

He removed my hand, positioned himself between my legs, and slammed into me. My head hit the headboard, which, for some reason, didn't hurt and only intensified the pleasure. I raised my hands over my head to steady myself as I wrapped my legs around his waist.

Using the headboard as leverage, I moved in motion with him as he plunged deeper and deeper. He lowered his head, capturing my lips in a kiss, and used an arm to grab my waist, lifting me higher. Our emotions intertwined and brought me closer to the edge.

He groaned as his body spasmed from an orgasm, causing one to erupt through me too. He stilled on top of me, kissing my cheek.

Egan's phone buzzed, and he moaned. "I should get that." He opened it and texted a reply. "It's Dad making sure you're okay. I called him when you were out."

"I heard you." I looked at the message and at the time. "Shit, my class starts in thirty minutes, and I need to grab something to eat." I wanted to go another round with him, but I didn't want to fall behind in my studies.

"Then we better take care of you." He stood without a moment's hesitation and pulled his clothes back on.

I stood there for a moment, taking in the view. I couldn't believe how lucky I was to have him as my mate. That word didn't make me wince. Progress.

"Are we in a hurry or not?" He sat on the bed and put on his shoes.

"Yes." I snapped out of it and got ready. "We are."

WE ENTERED THE STUDENT CENTER, and the loud noises and bright sights overwhelmed me. I could hear every individual conversation, and the lights were so bright they were almost blinding.

"Hey, are you okay?" Egan asked and pulled me out of the way of the foot traffic.

I got ready to reply then realized it wasn't the best idea. I tried projecting my thoughts toward him. *It's so loud and bright in here.* I wanted to cover my ears and close my eyes, but that would attract unwanted attention. *It's probably stupid, but it caught me off guard.*

It's not stupid at all. He frowned. *I should've thought about it. Why don't you go outside, and I'll get you something to eat. We can sit on a bench.*

It was freezing outside, but I'd rather be cold than inside here. *Okay, thank you.* I reached into my back pocket and pulled out some cash. *Here.*

Uh ... no. He kissed me and walked off. *This is on me.*

His emotions mixed with mine, conveying how important it was for him to take care of me, so I didn't say anything. Had it been just a few hours ago, I would've pressured him into taking my money. It was crazy to think how much had changed. Granted, I'd refuse to let him take care of everything for me, but maybe I could let him have some small victories from time to time.

As I walked outside, I braced myself for the chill, but it didn't come. The air was cool, but my body still felt warm. Normally, I'd be freezing already, but I could easily stand out here all day without a problem. I'd been so caught up with Egan that I hadn't realized it on our walk over.

"Hey, you," Sadie said, heading over to me. Her light pink hair sparkled in the sunlight, and she looked casually stylish as usual. She wore dark jeans and a white flowy shirt. "How are you doing?"

"I'm okay." I wasn't sure what to tell her. Did I just proclaim that Egan and I had sex and our bond had been formed? It was great to see that my social awkwardness was firmly intact. That weakness would've been nice to lose during the transition.

Standing a few feet away, she sniffed the air. Her mouth dropped open, and her eyes widened. "Oh my God. You and Egan—"

"—had sex." Why did I chime in? I must have wanted to make this moment as awkward as possible.

"Well, yeah." She laughed. "But I was going to say you finally got your acts together."

That was a better way of putting it. My face felt like it was on fire, and I glanced at the ground. "Yeah, I can't believe he waited for me. He was way more patient than I deserved."

"He would've waited forever for you." She somehow smiled bigger. "I'm just excited that you all worked through it so fast. You figured it out faster than Donovan and I did."

"Really?" That was hard to believe. They were so perfect together. I couldn't imagine them any other way.

"Are you two—" I paused and glanced around, making sure we were alone. "—mates too?"

"Yes, we are. It works similarly for us like it does for Egan's kind." She hugged me and then went still before pulling back. She tilted her head and squinted. "Or rather your kind. At first, I thought I was just smelling Egan, but that's you. How did he turn you?" she asked with an edge.

Of course, she'd ask that when he wasn't around. That was the secret he'd told me that no one outside of their race knew. "Uh ... he didn't, per se." I was brand spanking new to this and didn't want to start off by being the one with a big mouth. That wouldn't go over well with the other dragons.

The doors opened, and Egan walked out, carrying four biscuits and two cups of coffee. When his gaze landed on Sadie, he grimaced.

"What the hell is going on?" Sadie's eyes narrowed, and she crossed her arms. "What did you do to her? She's not herself anymore."

CHAPTER EIGHTEEN

Protectiveness surged through me. "Hey, don't talk to him like that." Sadie should know he would never do anything shady. I refused to let her imply he would.

Warmth radiated through our bond as Egan said, *It's fine. Let me talk to her. She's defending you in her own way.*

He walked over and handed me a biscuit and coffee. "It's not what you think." He winced and glanced around the courtyard. "Look, now isn't the best time to talk about this." He gestured to a group of students giving us strange looks as they walked past us.

Sadie stepped toward him, glaring. She wasn't giving the topic up. "Egan, she's different. Please tell me this isn't how you convinced her to stay with you."

"No, of course not." He flinched and stepped in front of me, blocking Sadie. "How could you think that?"

"Are you serious?" She pointed at me and sighed. "That's why. She's different from yesterday."

"I would never do anything against her will." He lowered his voice to barely above a whisper. "I told you the other day she would change when we completed the bond. This is what happens among my kind."

She sucked in a breath. "I had no clue you meant this."

This was the most uncomfortable situation I'd been in my entire life. My heart thawed toward her since she was sticking up for me, but I felt horrible for Egan. They were close, and I hated that I might've come between them. Keeping my mouth shut was extremely hard, but I understood why Egan wanted to handle it. This was a conversation more for them than for me. I got to be the bystander.

"Look, there's a lot about us you don't know." He took a deep breath like he was weighing each word, his attention on her. "And I haven't been at liberty to say, for many reasons. But things are changing. More of us will be rejoining society now."

"That's amazing news, but I wish you would've been more blunt about what we should expect. She's been around for a month, and it's just coming up. And yes, at one point, I didn't want you telling me things to protect yourself, but we're friends, and Tyler isn't part of the equation anymore." She motioned toward the dorms.

"There were many more reasons I couldn't share information with you beyond that." Egan sighed. "I had to protect my family."

"But you can trust us. We're all close, and you fought alongside me to take down Tyler. You know things about me that only our group knows. I get that you have your secrets, but something that affects us all is a huge deal."

"The keywords are 'fight alongside you.'" He inhaled sharply. "And I would do it all over again in a heartbeat. You're my best friends in the world, but my hands were tied until her. There is a lot to our history that no one realizes. You have to understand that she not only changed everything for me, but she also validated my whole reason for being here."

"It's hard to wrap my head around is all." Sadie shifted on her feet. "We knew you were full of secrets, but now I understand why you had no problems with Donovan being my mate when he was mostly human. You'd think supernaturals would remember that about dragons."

"We've been hiding for centuries." Egan leaned on his heels. "Like with all things, time has a way of erasing people's memories, and even then, we tried not to make it public knowledge.

"I am sorry you're hurt," he said sincerely. "That was never my intention, but a lot is at stake for my kind. We've stayed hidden for a reason."

"You're right." She exhaled shakily. "I'm being unreasonable, but I care about her too. This took me by surprise."

I glanced at my phone and frowned. "I hate to interrupt, but we need to head to class before we're late."

"Dammit," she grumbled. "I didn't get any breakfast."

"I can share half of this with you." I lifted the biscuit, hoping she'd say no. I kept my coffee securely in front of me. Even in friendship, I had to draw a line somewhere.

"Here." Egan handed Sadie one of his three biscuits. "Jade needs a meal after this morning."

Wow. He had to go there. First, his dad, and now Sadie. *Are you going to tell everyone we had sex? Should I be thankful you didn't say twice?*

He faced me, and his eyes glowed faintly as he smirked. *I was referring to the change, not being intimate.*

Yeah, I knew that, I lied, and a horrible stench hit my nose. I gagged. "What the hell is that smell?"

"I have no clue what you two were talking about." Sadie

waved her free hand in front of her nose. "But I know you just told a huge lie."

"Wait ..." My stomach dropped. "Lying smells?"

Egan was smart enough to pretend he wasn't smiling. "Yeah, and the person's heartbeat increases, so you can hear and smell it from most everybody. There's only one person I've heard of who could lie without anyone knowing."

"Yup." Sadie visibly shook. "The man who I thought was my father for most of my life. He was a lying piece of shit."

How she felt about him was clear. "You knew every time I lied to you?" I cringed, trying to remember what I'd said.

"I liked smelling you lie when you'd deny your attraction to me." He winked. "And don't forget the time you lied to me about having a backpack."

Oh my God. No wonder it had looked like he'd smelled something bad. It had been my lie. Thankfully, I hadn't stunk.

"Let's go," Sadie said and gestured to Egan's coffee. "You aren't willing to give that up as well, are you?"

"Here you go." He handed her the drink, turned, and kissed me. *Just know I refuse to kiss and tell. I only called my dad because I thought something was wrong. I would never disrespect you like that even though those two times have been running through my mind constantly.*

Heat shot through my body. *We'll need a repeat performance and soon.*

"Also, people can smell arousal." Sadie wrinkled her nose. "And here I thought Roxy and Axel were bad."

"Does it smell spicy?" Maybe that was what I'd smelled when Egan and I had sex the second time.

"Yes, it does." He chuckled. He pulled me against him

and kissed my lips one more time. "Now go. I'll grab some more breakfast and see you in Spanish class in an hour."

As I walked away, I could feel his eyes on me, and I licked my lips, enjoying his taste. At least, those were fewer calories than cinnamon rolls and way more delicious. I swayed my hips a bit more for his viewing pleasure.

Jade, he warned. *You won't be going to class if you keep doing that.*

A chuckle escaped before I could stop it.

"You look really happy." Sadie grinned, but her forehead lined with worry. "I'm glad, but how are you? I can't imagine how you're feeling."

"I'm actually really happy." It'd been so long, I'd almost forgotten what happiness felt like.

"I'm glad, but that's not what I meant." She kept her focus forward. "I meant, how are you feeling?"

We passed a few girls on the sidewalk, and I realized she was speaking in code. "A little out of sorts, but stronger than ever before." Staring into the woods, I could see each individual leaf a hundred feet away. No matter where I looked, it was like I was staring through a microscope. I blinked, but the strength of my vision didn't lessen.

"I bet." Sadie blew out a breath. "Donovan had a hard time too."

My body stiffened, and I was thankful no one was within hearing distance. "Donovan was human? Did he change after you completed the bond too?" I'd figured all of them had been born this way.

"Mostly human, but he had a little shifter in him." She adjusted her backpack on her shoulders. "Tyler had a vampire try to kill him and Axel. Roxy and I found them and bit them, initiating their transformation into a full wolf."

"Whoa. Is Tyler the one you thought was your father?" He sounded like someone my aunt would get along with.

"Yup, and he wanted me to be with someone else, so he tried to kill Donovan to force my hand." She rolled her eyes. "It was ridiculous. Needless to say, he wouldn't let it go. Then, I found out he wasn't my real dad. Tyler actually had my dad imprisoned. Last semester was a huge mess."

Boy, did it sound like it. "Is everything good now?"

"Yeah." She took a sip of her coffee. "It's been really good. Dad and I are getting to know each other, and Tyler is no longer a threat. Things are settling, and I must say I'm the happiest I've ever been too."

"Is your dad fae or shifter?" Her being a hybrid had piqued my curiosity. I wondered how common that was.

"He's fae." She looked skyward, deep in thought. "He's teaching me how to connect with that side of me and control it. Since there aren't many hybrids, I have to learn each side of me separately then figure out how to make each side work together. It's challenging but in a good way."

"Wow, I thought there would be more hybrids in the world."

"No." She shook her head. "We're a segregated bunch. Our friend group is unique. We're hoping to help bridge the gap between the races. We all may be different, but we have a lot in common. Hell, if the humans can do it, so can we."

As we approached the building, Sadie stopped me several feet away from everyone. She bit her bottom lip. "Egan's a great guy, and I'm ecstatic to see you two together, but I need to hear it from you. Did he tell you before you completed the bond?"

"Yes, he did." He'd told me in the heat of the moment, but he had tried to get me to slow down. "I made the choice, not him."

"Good." She nodded, and her shoulders relaxed. "Donovan didn't get that choice, and it's something I still feel guilty about to this day."

"Why?" She'd saved him. There was no reason for her to feel guilty.

"Like I said, he struggled at first," she said and headed to the door. "He wasn't thrilled with what I'd done, but he came around, thankfully. The problem with biting someone to change them is that less than one percent of people survive the change, and the ones who do have abnormalities like not being able to see or hear. What I did was risky, but him and Axel already being part animal prevented those issues from occurring. That's another reason I freaked out. Something could've happened to you."

"You did the right thing. And I'm perfectly fine. I appreciate your concern." I would've done the same thing had I been in her position. "And it obviously worked out for both of us."

"It did." But the smile left her face. "I got lucky, but I learned something that day. Everyone should be given the choice, and that's why it's important to me that he gave you that option."

"He's taken care of me since the moment we met," I assured her. "He tried to talk me out of doing it so fast."

"I'm not surprised. He's a true gentleman." She bumped her shoulder into mine. "I'm glad we're stuck with you. Now, we'd better get to class. It's about to start."

My CLASSES PASSED in slow motion. Spanish felt like pure torture with Egan sitting so close yet still too far away. I couldn't pay attention while his scent and memories of this morning ran through my head. The spicy edge to his scent alerted me that he was struggling as well, which ramped me up even more. We were feeding off each other in very inappropriate ways.

As soon as class ended, Egan stood and carried both his and my backpacks. He took my hand, and I felt as if our souls were connected.

We walked in comfortable silence. Outside, I reached for my bag.

"I've got it," he said as he dodged my hand.

"You've got another class." I stepped closer to his side, enjoying how close he was. "Are you planning on taking two bags to class?"

"Nope." He kissed my cheek and winked. "I'm skipping class to spend more time with my love."

My heart soared at the word, but I didn't make a big deal out of it. It was a pet name, not a proclamation of his love for me. "You missed Friday too." I purposely left out the fact it had been due to my horrible attitude.

"So?" He wrapped his arm around my waist, managing to balance both bags on his shoulders. "It almost killed me to be away from you earlier. I need the rest of the day with you right next to me."

"At least, you changed clothes in that hour," I teased. "You wore your other clothes several days in a row."

"Don't remind me." He led me past the Student Center and straight to the women's dorm. "But I showered and trimmed." He rubbed the scruff on his chin. "And I need some alone time with you before we have to meet up with the others for lunch."

"Alone time?" The thought already had my body primed and ready. "I guess if I have to ..."

"Oh, you have to." His smile made him so damn breathtaking.

Just from this morning, I impossibly felt so much more for him. He was everything I'd ever wanted or needed. "Fine, but only because I don't want to hurt your feelings."

"It would hurt them, all right."

My cheeks hurt from smiling so much, but I was giddy. Nothing could bring me down from my high.

We rushed into the women's dorm and were in my room within seconds. He dropped the bags to the floor and grabbed my ass, lifting me into the air. I wrapped my legs around his waist as he carried me over to the bed.

His lips captured mine, and I moaned as our tongues tangled together. His fingers kneaded my ass before he lowered me gently onto the mattress and released his hold. I whimpered in desperation. I didn't want him to stop touching me.

Aggravated, I climbed to my feet and pushed him so he sat on the bed. I straddled him and rocked against him, feeling his hardness.

All of my senses were locked on him as he cupped my breast, rubbing my nipple through my shirt. I grabbed the hem of my shirt to pull it off me when I heard footsteps approaching our door.

Of all times, Vera had decided to come back now. Right as I pulled back to stand, the door opened.

"What the hell?" Vera gasped.

CHAPTER NINETEEN

My roommate had walked in on Egan and me, making my skin crawl. I'd never imagined anything like this would happen to me. Prior to coming here, I'd been determined to never get close to anyone, yet here I was, close to him both physically and emotionally.

I jumped to my feet and closed my eyes. "I'm so sorry. You've been gone, and you normally have class right now."

"Uh ..." She held her worn leather binder close to her heart. "Yeah, I have been." Her attention shifted to Egan, and she frowned. "I thought you two weren't together."

Wow, as if this could get even more uncomfortable. "We weren't." I glanced at Egan, at a loss as to what to say.

"But this weekend, I convinced her to give me a shot." Egan smiled adoringly at me. "I had to wear her down, but I'd do it all over again in a heartbeat."

"This weekend?" Vera scowled. "You've been together all weekend?"

She hated me eating in the room, so she must not be thrilled about sex. "We didn't fornicate on your side of the room."

Egan chuckled and tried to cover it up with a cough. *Fornicate?*

When I get uncomfortable, things just fall out of my mouth. Sarah hated when I did that, which would just make me more nervous, and I'd say even more outlandish things. She'd eventually avoided taking me out in public at all costs.

Like telling a guy, who was trying to buy their mate's schoolbooks, that she wouldn't have sex or provide blow jobs in the form of payment? he teased.

Yeah, that wasn't my finest moment. Finding him super attractive didn't help matters either. *But yes, my point exactly. And in all fairness, I didn't know we were soul mates. Here I thought you were a gentleman and wouldn't make fun of me.*

Oh, stop. He grabbed my waist and pulled me against his chest. *I'm just teasing.*

Vera cleared her throat. "That's such a relief," she spat. She was more pissed than I'd guessed.

"Look, this is my room too." I wasn't about to apologize for having my mate in my dorm. "I have a right to have people in here too." Things had gone well until now. We didn't talk much, and she kept to her side.

"Why don't you have sex in his room?" She marched over to her desk, opened the bottom drawer, and threw her grandmother's journal into it.

She was usually so careful with it, and her reaction caught me off guard. "Because my roommate wasn't around." I realized I'd never been to his room, but that wasn't completely strange. We'd become official not even twenty-four hours ago.

"Well, I'm back." She crossed her arms, giving me a wicked death glare. Her nerdy attitude was completely gone, replaced with one of a complete and utter bitch. "So he can leave. Now."

"Are you serious?" Her rage made no sense. Sure, I could see how she'd be a little upset over what she'd walked in on, but she was livid.

"Sadie and the others are probably at the Student Center." Egan stood and intertwined our fingers. "Let's go eat some lunch and give her time to get settled after being gone all weekend." *It's not worth upsetting her more than she already is.*

I wanted to stand my ground, but I'd learned to choose my battles. Hmm ... I was still considered a person, right? *Things* didn't seem appropriate. More questions for me to ponder. "Yeah, okay." I didn't want the rest of my year to be unpleasant, so I'd suck it up. *Give me a second?*

Of course. He kissed my cheek and let go of my hand. "I'll give you two a chance to talk and wait out in the hallway."

Vera stood in front of her desk, glaring at him the entire time he walked out the door. As soon as the door shut, she faced me. "That is not something I ever want to walk in on again."

"Look." I paused to collect myself and not react irrationally. "I'm sorry. Believe me when I say I'd rather you hadn't walked in on that either." In fact, I'd rather fall and skin my knee and have blood pouring all down my leg and into my shoe. Like legit, this was mortifying, and the way she was acting made it worse.

Her body remained tense, but she dropped her arms. "It just caught me off guard. The last time I tried talking to you about him, you ran out the door."

"I know." Ugh, I hadn't meant to hurt her feelings. "We have this connection that scared me."

"Really?" She lifted an eyebrow. "What kind of connection? Sexual?" She chuckled.

"Real funny." This was the most personable conversation we'd had. She either asked questions I didn't want to answer or had a nose buried in a book. "But it's more than that." Fated mates didn't even describe the magnitude of my feelings, but I couldn't use that term with her since she was human. "I'm drawn to him, and being with him makes me feel whole."

"Interesting." She tapped a finger on her bottom lip. "Well, that's amazing." Her words lacked enthusiasm.

"I'll get out of here so you can get settled in." Her less-than-thrilled reaction told me I needed to give her time to deal with whatever had happened this weekend. This reaction couldn't have been over her walking in on us. "Is everything okay? You left without a word, and your clothes were thrown everywhere."

"Yeah." She glanced at the door. "I wanted to take care of some things, but I couldn't get it finished." She shrugged. "I'll get it right next time."

"That sucks." I opened the door and glanced over my shoulder. "At least, you know what you're up against."

"Very true." She opened the drawer that held the leather book and turned her back to me.

She'd dismissed me, and that was perfectly okay with me. I rushed out the door and found two girls talking to Egan. I'd never noticed them before, but that wasn't saying much. I wasn't a social butterfly and usually avoided looking into people's eyes. I didn't want them to see I wanted to talk or was staring at them.

The girl with bleached blonde hair touched his arm. Egan moved to get her to drop her hand, but the hussy stepped with him, keeping her hand firmly in place.

Raw anger flowed through me. I'd never been this angry in my entire life. I marched over and removed her hand while purring, "Hey, baby."

His eyes lightened to liquid gold. "Hey, you." He kissed me right in front of the girls, helping me stake my claim.

"Oh." The other girl tossed her caramel hair over her shoulder. "I thought you were waiting on a friend. I didn't realize—"

"Now you do." A roar sounded inside me, startling me. The only plausible explanation was that the noise had come from my dragon.

"She's the only one for me." He pulled away and cupped my cheek. *Your eyes are glowing. Calm down.* But the corner of his mouth tilted up.

I'm sorry. I tried focusing on him and forgetting about the two girls, but I couldn't. *It's like I can't shut it down.*

Your dragon is going crazy. He hugged me, pulling me flush against his chest. *Between changing less than a day ago and the new mate bond, your animal side is a little more in control.*

Having his arms wrapped around me and breathing him in worked its magic. I buried my face into his chest.

Egan took my hand and tugged me toward the elevator. "You two have a good afternoon."

As I walked by them, I glared, not wanting to leave, and Egan wrapped an arm around me to help my legs move. His shoulders shook against my arm. He clearly enjoyed my jealous fit of rage. If I hadn't been so angry, I probably would've found it funny too.

A frown remained firmly locked in place as we entered the Student Center. Egan ushered me toward his friends, who had their usual two tables pushed together. Axel and Donovan sat on the end across from each other with their

188 JEN L. GREY

mates right next to them. Katherine sat next to Roxy, and Lillith sat next to Sadie.

Roxy grinned and said loudly, "Look who we've got here. I almost thought they wouldn't come."

"Do you not smell the amount of horniness pouring off them?" Lillith whispered loudly. "You think they would've taken care of that before joining us so we wouldn't all lose our appetites smelling that." She lifted her drink.

That was enough to snap me back to reality and forget those two girls. I jerked my head in their direction and wanted to disappear.

"We got her attention now." Roxy leaned back in her seat and nodded to Sadie. "So, Sadie informed us that you all"—she lifted one hand, made it a circle, then inserted her pointer finger into the hole.

Lillith took a sip of the blood hidden in her coffee mug. "Be careful which way you point the circle. I think if you turn the hand so the fingers are closer to a heart shape, it represents the anus."

"What?" Katherine choked. "Are you serious?"

I'd never been so damn embarrassed before, but if I hid, it would only encourage her.

"Roxy," Egan warned. *She enjoys making people feel uncomfortable. I'm sorry. If it's any consolation, Sadie and I became friends first. She was part of the package deal.*

"Just ignore them. She has to be making that up." Sadie didn't sound so sure. "Either way, I informed them that you completed the bond. I didn't call out sex specifically."

Donovan sighed and shook his head. "You know how Roxy's mind works. Are you really surprised?"

"So." Roxy waggled her eyebrows and took a huge bite of her pizza. "How many times have you all made it official?"

Axel groaned. "Leave her alone. If you scare her off, I'll have to hear Egan whine and cry about her again. It was brutal. Don't make me relive that."

Egan scowled at the vibrant redhead. "Let's go get something to eat so those two can calm down." He pointed right at Lillith then Roxy.

"Oh, stop." Sadie stood and snatched my arm. "Lillith, will you go sit by Katherine so Jade and Egan can sit next to each other?"

"Fine." She grabbed her drink and walked around us. "But only because they're new to their *relationship* and I don't want to hear them complain." She winked at me, letting me know she was kidding.

"Come sit next to me while Egan grabs your food." Sadie sat back in her place and patted the spot next to her. "I promise I'll make them behave." She stared pointedly at Roxy.

"I'll behave." Roxy pouted, but her hazel eyes were alight with mirth. "But only because I like her."

It finally sank in. I had an actual group of friends. For the first time in my life, I felt complete.

———

BEFORE I REALIZED IT, it was Friday. I walked out of Spanish class and was heading to my dorm when the tingling feeling overtook me. The feeling had gotten so bad any time I wasn't around Egan; I felt like I was being watched even when I was in my dorm room at night.

Thankfully, I'd gotten a hold on projecting my thoughts quickly. I didn't want Egan to worry about me more than he already did.

It had to be paranoia just like when I first got here. The

feeling had eased for a little while, but the past week had been almost unbearable. If Egan hadn't already missed so many classes, I would've asked him to walk me back to the dorm. That was something I would've refused a week ago, thinking it made me weak, but I was learning that asking for help wasn't a weakness.

Overcoming the urge to run, I walked briskly across campus. Within minutes, I made it to my room and shut and locked the door.

Vera and I hadn't argued since the Monday mishap, but our relationship was strained. She'd tried talking to me the other night again, but the topic had centered around Egan. Don't get me wrong, I loved talking and thinking about him, just not with her or anyone outside our friend group.

Luckily, I was acclimating to my dragon, but she was probably making my paranoia skyrocket. The sensations were intense, so I had to be reading into stuff that wasn't there.

Despite those thoughts, I marched over to the window and shut the blinds. Darkness or light, my vision never changed, but if someone was watching me, they couldn't see through the plastic.

Even with the blinds closed, that nagging feeling tugged on my subconscious. My skin crawled, and my dragon shifted uncomfortably inside me. Maybe I needed to talk to Egan after his class and tell him what was going on. It made me feel like I was going insane.

Trying to distract my racing mind, I pulled my phone from my pocket and opened Messenger. I'd avoided logging in for the past week, and I had ten new messages from Mom. She begged to know where I was and if I was okay. I had a feeling Sarah was pushing for a location.

I quickly tapped out a reply, telling her not to worry and

that I was fine. I hadn't told her that I'd left to attend college. That would have narrowed down the possibilities of where to find me.

Once I was done messaging her, my focus landed on Vera's desk. She'd been clutching her grandmother's journal more since she returned from wherever the hell she'd gone to. What could be so important in that thing? She rarely left it behind, but if the journal was here, maybe I could find out what was so special.

My dragon brushed across my mind, and the urge to look at it intensified. One quick look wouldn't be a big deal. If nothing seemed odd, she'd be none the wiser. But for her to be that attached to it, something special had to be involved.

I stood and slowly walked over to the desk, quiet as a mouse. She wasn't in the room, but it felt like she could easily catch me. Instead of questioning those feelings, I tiptoed over. As I touched the handle of the drawer, a bird cried outside my window.

My body stilled, and something crashed into the glass.

CHAPTER TWENTY

No way. A bird couldn't be trying to break through my window. That had to be a coincidence.

Another *kak* sounded, and the bird slammed into the window again. A faint crack in the window made my stomach drop.

Holy shit. A bird really was doing that. The shock was enough to drop the barrier I'd put up between Egan and me.

The bird hit the window again and again, and the glass fractured even more.

What's wrong? His concern was evident in his tone. *Are you okay?*

I'm not sure. I couldn't lie to him. I stood as snooping through Vera's desk had become way less of a priority. *A bird is trying to crash through the window of my dorm.*

I'll be there in a flash.

I was slightly relieved that he was on his way, but I wasn't out of the situation. I braced for the bird to hit again, but nothing happened.

Day by day, things seemed to get more bizarre.

When everything remained silent, I crept across the

room toward my bed. I placed my knee on the mattress and leaned toward the blinds. I peeked through and came face to face with a falcon.

I screamed bloody murder and stumbled back as the door burst open. Egan raced into the room and pulled me against his chest.

"What's wrong?' He pushed me behind him. "I heard you scream."

"Uh ... no." I moved around him. "We can face the threat together, thank you." I liked that he wanted to protect me but hated that he thought I couldn't protect myself. I felt all confused inside. At the end of the day, I needed him to treat me as an equal, but that was a conversation for another time.

"Jade, what happened?" he asked with frustration.

"A bird slammed into my window over and over again. Then it just stopped." I rubbed my arms. "I peeked through the blinds, and a falcon was there just staring at me." It had to be the bird that had killed at least one of those girls, if not Amber too. "I think it's gone. I don't hear anything now."

He opened the blinds, and as I suspected, the falcon was no longer there. A deep, long crack marred the glass, proving I hadn't lost my mind.

"What were you doing when it happened?" He ran his finger along the crack. "Luckily, it's only on the outside and not broken inside, but it had to hit it hard to accomplish this."

"You're telling me." That bird had wanted in. "And I was over by Vera's desk. I ... wanted to check something out." That sounded much better than coming right out and saying I was snooping.

"I don't like this." Egan frowned. "My roommate is

going home for the weekend. You can stay with me until the school fixes this window."

That thrilled me, but why hadn't he told me that sooner? Maybe he hadn't wanted me to stay with him. "No, it's fine. I don't want to impose." I tried to keep the hurt from my voice.

"Uh ... it's no imposition." His forehead wrinkled. "In fact, I kind of demand it. Ever since I learned about his leaving this morning, my thoughts have been consumed with us spending the whole weekend locked in my room. I'm thinking we order in so we don't have to leave."

"Now that sounds like a plan I can get behind." Then I remembered. "But I have to work nights at Haynes."

"What?" Egan's face fell. "No. Why don't you quit?"

"Excuse me?" I'd been letting him buy me lunches because he always ran off to get it while the girls talked to me, but I didn't want him to become my sugar daddy. "No, I need money to support myself."

"First off, you don't need to worry about money anymore. I'll take care of you."

"I don't want to be a mooch." The thought of relying on someone else for everything scared me. "I need some independence."

He flinched.

"Not independence like that." Damn, I really needed to work on my communication skills. "I don't want to ask for money if I need something."

"Yeah, I get that." He nodded, although his lips turned downward. "But that's not the main reason. Remember when I came into Haynes last Friday?"

"Oh, that's something I'll never forget." Amber had been all over him, and later, she'd wound up dead. I'd wanted to hurt her, but I never would have wished death on her. "I had to leave early, remember?"

"Yeah, I remember." He brushed my cheek. "But I haven't told you the real reason I showed up there."

"I'm all ears." Patience was not my best virtue.

"Give me a second." He chuckled. "Now that you know about us, I can tell you. We're tracking the falcon that's been attacking people."

"Yeah, that bird has lost its mind." I gestured to my window. "It had to be him."

"It was. I recognize the scent, but there's more to the story than that." He closed the blinds. "It's a falcon shifter."

"Wait ... are all birds shifters?" I hadn't considered the possibility that all animals were shifters.

"No. Only falcons and crows, but not every one of them is necessarily a shifter." He shrugged. "The others are true animals."

"So someone is using his animal form to attack and kill girls." A chill ran down my spine. "That's pretty morbid. What about animal control? They'll kill him if they find him."

"He shifts back into his human form, and no one is the wiser." He pointed back and forth between us. "Except for supernaturals like us."

That was still strange to hear. Being something other than human was taking a bit to get used to. Maybe because I hadn't shifted before. Then the memory of the woods settled over me. "Wait ... that day when you found me in the woods, running for my life, I could have sworn I heard someone chuckle as they chased me, but I thought I was losing my mind."

"It was the bird." Egan tensed. "He was after you. I don't know what would've happened if I hadn't found you when I did. But whoever it is was hanging around at Haynes. Their scent was all over the place. You can't go back there."

"First off, it's my choice." I tried to calm the annoyance he'd stirred up. "And second, I can't leave them high and dry. I did that last weekend. I have to put in a notice." If he was concerned for my safety, that was something completely different from wanting me not to work.

He hung his head. "Fine, but I'm going with you. I'll take a seat at the bar and keep out of sight as well as possible."

I crossed my arms and lifted my chin. "But if a girl touches you, I can't be held liable for my reaction."

"I'll make sure no one touches me." He kissed me, and the rest of my worries melted away.

"ARE you sure you don't want to call in?" Egan asked for the tenth time. He sat on his bed, watching me pull my work clothes on. My body was still warm from the sex we'd just had.

"I have to." His dorm room was the same as mine. It was obvious that both buildings had been built at the same time with the same layout. The only difference was that Egan's scent was everywhere, and his dark blue sheets smelled like heaven. I could easily get used to waking up with him every day. "Besides, you have Donovan and Sadie coming too."

At lunch, he'd asked them to join us in case we'd need backup. Apparently, Lillith and Axel would hang out in the back alley while Katherine and Roxy would wait out front in a car. They felt certain that whoever was hurting these girls either went to Haynes to stalk his prey or, even scarier, worked there.

A knock sounded on the door, and Donovan's and Sadie's scents hit my nose.

"You ready?" I faced him, arching an eyebrow.

"One second," he called and wrinkled his nose at me. He stood in his naked glory and grabbed his clothes from the floor.

I leaned back against the wall and enjoyed watching him dress.

Like what you see? He pulled up his pants as he thrust his ass out. He was so muscular it didn't jiggle.

Before mating with him, I wouldn't have believed he had this playful side. It came out in spurts, and he could make me laugh like never before. *Maybe. But instead of trying to make your ass jiggle ...* I trailed off while lifting my eyebrows suggestively.

Keep looking at me like that and you won't make it to work. He threatened good-naturedly. *And you won't be allowed to complain about it.*

My body was ready for another round. I didn't realize I'd be so sexually charged, but I couldn't get enough of him.

"Okay, I wish Roxy were around," Donovan grumbled. "I can smell them from out here."

Sadie giggled. "Leave them alone. I'm just happy Egan found someone so great."

A smile spread across my face.

Egan walked over to me and took my hand. He kissed me quickly and said, *I agree with her completely.* He opened the door, revealing Sadie and Donovan.

Sadie had on dressy black slacks and a baby-blue top that contrasted with her hair. Donovan wore his usual jeans and a black t-shirt. He had an arm wrapped around his mate.

"You two ready?" she asked.

"Yeah, I'm scheduled to start in fifteen minutes, so we'd better haul ass."

"Then we'd better go." Egan pulled his car keys out of his pocket, and we headed down to the first floor.

In the parking lot, I realized I'd never seen Egan's vehicle before, but when he led me to a new maroon Jeep, I wasn't surprised. The car fit him perfectly.

"Here you go." Egan opened the front passenger seat and helped me inside.

"Yo," Roxy called out as she, Axel, and the two vampires headed our way. "Are you not going to wait for us?"

"The whole point was to arrive separately in case anyone is watching." Sadie rolled her eyes. "So, no, we weren't planning on waiting on you."

"Fine." Roxy sighed and wrapped her arms around Lillith and Katherine. "They waited for me."

"Because we had to." Lillith shook her head. "At least, I won't be stuck with you once we get there. That would be a disaster."

I'd been surprised that Roxy and Axel wouldn't stay together, but Egan had explained that they were splitting up because of their pack link. That way, someone from their pack would be with each group and could easily communicate if something went down.

"We really need to go." I hated to be late. I'd promised Egan I would turn my notice in tonight since he felt like I was in danger there. I had no desire to relive that moment with the creepy bird shifter.

"Remember to blend in." Donovan glared at Roxy then Lillith. "Especially you two."

"I feel attacked," Roxy huffed.

Lillith pursed her lips. "You do realize they didn't put us together for a reason?"

"Are you surprised?" Katherine pulled at her navy blue top.

"Nope." Lillith pouted. "A very smart call on their part."

Axel sighed. "At least, I'll be with the accountable one."

"Hey." Roxy punched him in the arm. "I'm your mate and standing right here."

"Of course, I want you." He widened his eyes at Donovan. "Not her."

"Uh ... I'm right here too." Lillith placed a hand on her hip.

"Good luck, man." Donovan laughed and shut the door.

Soon, Egan pulled out of the parking spot, leaving the four of them behind. The entire ride to the steakhouse passed in silence. Whether anyone wanted to admit it, we were all on edge. My skin itched like something was going to happen, but my dragon couldn't sense that ... right?

When the restaurant appeared, I brushed off my anticipation to focus on the task at hand. The first order of business was clocking in and giving Ollie my notice. I just needed to go in and rip the Band-Aid off. Then I could begin searching for another job.

The four of us entered the building, and Betty was behind the desk.

"Hi. How many are in your party?" she asked, her eyes locked on Egan.

If I hadn't known better, I would've thought I was a wolf shifter. The urge to pee on Egan's leg was awfully strong. "Three, and please sit them in my section." I kissed Egan's lips and winked. "I'll come get your order soon." I turned and sashayed away, feeling his eyes focused on my ass.

I headed toward the back and caught Ollie marching to the back of the kitchen. He hated going back there. Odd.

"Hey, Ollie." I increased my pace. "Wait up."

He paused and turned to face me. "What's up? I'm in a hurry."

Well, okay then, I'd cut to the chase. "I wanted to let you know that this weekend is the last one I'll be working."

"Aw, really?" His shoulders sagged. "That's a damn shame. But at least we have you for this weekend." He spun back around and continued toward the back.

Okay, that was easy and strange. But hell, after that bird attack, I'd take it. I went to work and found Egan, Sadie, and Donovan seated in the back section of the restaurant.

I hurried over with my pad and pen. "What can I get you all?"

"Waters for all of us," Egan said, scanning the room. *He's here again.*

I hadn't caught the scent yet since my dragon side formed, so I had no clue what to look for. *Are the others here yet?*

Yeah. He touched my arm. *They're getting in position. They pulled up a few minutes ago.*

That made me feel a little better. I forced a smile and nodded. "I'll go get your drinks and come back for your order."

I walked to the drink station and was filling the waters when a server hurried over to me.

She glanced over her shoulder toward the kitchen. "For some reason, Ollie needs your help. He said it's about one of your table orders."

Ugh, I'd just taken over Chad's shift, and there was

already an issue. "Okay, thanks. I'll go back there now." I placed the water on the table and rushed toward the back. The cooks were all busy with no sign of Ollie. I glanced toward the back door and saw him standing there with a phone in his hand.

I marched over. None of this made sense. If an order was wrong, he'd be with the cooks. I opened my mouth to say, "Hey," when he looked at me and blew powder in my face. The room began to spin, and my legs wobbled.

CHAPTER TWENTY-ONE

I tried connecting with Egan, but my head was swimming too much. My own thoughts were nearly unintelligible.

"Are you drunk on the job?" Ollie scoffed and wrapped an arm around my waist. "I can't believe the audacity."

My legs wouldn't hold my weight, and my body sagged against him like he was helping me. For anyone watching, his accusation looked believable. Everything inside me told me to push away, but his arm was tight around my waist.

Could Ollie be the falcon shifter? Surely not. But why else would he be doing this? Others had quit, and they hadn't wound up hurt the next day or weeks later.

"Guys, I have to take her home," Ollie told the cooks. "If anyone is looking for me, tell them I'll be back when I can."

The older cook nodded as he frowned. "Yeah, get her out of here. I don't need her puking back here. The last thing we need is the health department hearing about that."

Ollie opened the back door and tugged me outside. My feet couldn't move, tripping me. I was so out of it I couldn't even groan. Something inside me screamed to yell for help or connect with Egan, but I couldn't function. I wasn't sure how I was even breathing.

The dusky sky hit my eyes as my gaze settled on a black sedan parked in the back. The driver's door opened, revealing the occupant. My stomach roiled when I saw her face.

It was Vera.

My own fucking roommate.

Why would she be here?

"Get her inside." She opened the back driver's side door, gesturing for Ollie to hurry. "Those other two will be here any second." She wore all black, making her words sound even more ominous.

I'd never felt so betrayed. We'd never been close, but this was cold. What had I ever done to make her want to hurt me? Had sex while she was out of town? What was worse was that she knew who Axel and Lillith were. That meant she'd been watching me. Could she be the reason I'd felt constantly watched?

"She's dead weight," he groaned and threw me over his shoulder.

My head hung, giving me a view of his scrawny ass. Definitely not the last sight I wanted to see before croaking. Maybe this was part of their torture.

"Hurry," she hissed as Ollie carried me over. As he tossed me in the car, Axel and Lillith rounded the corner.

Lillith's eyes widened, but then I landed in the car, and all I could see was the light tan leather of the seat and the tan floorboard.

"Get in the car!" Vera said loudly as she slammed the back door. Within seconds, the passenger door opened as they got in. There was a bang on the glass above my head, followed by the squealing of tires as Vera punched the gas.

"Dammit." She turned the car sharply. "We were supposed to be farther away before they realized she was gone."

"I'm sorry," Ollie huffed. "But I got her as soon as I could." He didn't sound thrilled.

Jade? Egan sounded half-crazed. *Are you okay?*

Ugh. My grunt was the only response I could manage, but it was better than what I could do a few minutes ago. *Veewwwaaa.* And I sounded like a toddler, but I considered that a huge win.

Your roommate? Horror pulsed through our bond. *She's with you. Is she okay?*

Great, now he thought we were both in danger. I didn't want to say anything in case it made things worse.

Don't worry, he reassured me. *We'll find you. I can follow our bond. It might just take a minute before I can get there, but I'm on my way.*

I didn't realize he could track the mate bond, but hell, I didn't know much. I hadn't been a supernatural long—not even a week.

"What are we going to do?" Anxiety wafted off Ollie. "They'll be hunting us now."

"Nothing changes." Vera sounded resolved. "Our plan is still intact."

"You're playing a dangerous game." Ollie sounded tense. "And you've got more people at risk than yourself."

"It doesn't matter what you think," she spat. "I'm the one who makes the call, or should I remind you why?"

That was enough to shut him up.

I wiggled my fingers, and my thoughts began to clear. Whatever they'd done to me was wearing off, but I had to be careful. I didn't need them knowing.

Silence descended as we traveled farther and farther

away from the restaurant. I should've realized that Ollie's creepy behavior had something to do with this, and Vera had gotten way too upset about Egan and me the other day. All of these red flags, and I'd ignored them. I'd figured she'd been upset about something that she'd done that weekend, but maybe there was more to it than that.

Egan? I linked with him, hoping I was clear enough to understand. Thankfully, I sounded almost normal again. *Are you there?*

Yes. Are you okay?

I'm not sure how to answer that. I wasn't hurt, but I was far from okay. *Vera and Ollie kidnapped me.*

She helped kidnap you? He sounded surprised but not completely shocked. Regret flowed between us. *I picked up vibes from her, but I didn't think it would be something like this.* He paused. *What did they do to you? Lillith said it looked like you were paralyzed.*

That was the million-dollar question. *I have no clue. Ollie blew something into my face, and I went completely slack. I almost fell to the ground. He told the cooks I was drunk and he needed to take me home. Vera was out back waiting for us with the car.*

I had a bad feeling something would happen tonight. She has to be a witch, which makes sense given the leather journal we saw the other day. She used a spell on you. He growled through the bond. *We're looking for you, but it's hard since you're a moving target. Are you still on the road? Can you tell us anything about your surroundings?*

No, I can't. The car took a turn, and I adjusted my head ever so slightly. Ollie glanced back immediately, and I went completely still.

Please, God, don't let him realize I moved my head. He frowned but said nothing.

DRAGON MATE   207

I can't risk trying to look around. I'm trying to look like the spell is still working. Add that to the list of things I never imagined I'd say. *But we're taking some sharp turns.*

That tells me you're heading out of downtown. He sounded so distraught. *When you get there, tell me anything you can see. Axel is right behind us. We're all heading that way.*

I hated that I hadn't listened to him. In hindsight, demanding to turn in my notice had been stupid. I'd thought he was being overly paranoid, though. He tended to get very protective, so I'd brushed it off as just that. Apparently, I needed to trust his instincts more and realize he wasn't trying to stifle me. *I'll let you know if I figure out anything.*

He sighed. *Please, be safe. I can't lose you.*

The words "I love you" almost projected into our bond, but I bit my tongue. I refused to tell him that for the first time in a situation like this. I had to make it out alive and tell him in person.

Time crept by, and I had no clue how long we'd been driving. Eventually, she turned again, and the car bounced as we crunched over gravel. We had to be approaching our destination.

We're slowing down. This would give him some indication of how far we'd traveled, which should aid them in their search for me. *I'll let you know what I can see when they get me out.*

"Do you think they're tracking her?" Ollie asked, almost scaring me.

The car had been silent for so long. I managed to clamp down my reaction, keeping up the act of not being able to control my body.

"No, the spell should block them," Vera said as the car

came to a stop. "We should have a few hours before it wears off, so plenty of time."

"I hope you're right." Ollie exhaled and opened his door. "I'll bring her inside."

A few seconds later, the door opened, and Ollie placed his hands under my arm, tugging me toward him. I remained dead weight and took a deep, calming breath. If I moved, there was no telling what they would do.

He grunted as he dragged me toward him and turned me over so I was facing the roof. He leaned over, grasped my upper body, and threw me over his shoulder again. Before he could straighten, my head bounced against the top part of his ass. I squinted, trying to forget the up-close view I had of his ass cheeks.

"What's taking so long?" Vera sounded unhinged. "Get her in here now."

"I'm trying." He stood and hurried toward the log cabin.

As my body jarred, I took in as much of my surroundings as I could. *We're at an older log cabin. I can't get a good view of it from my position, but it looks like we're in the middle of the woods with no nearby neighbors.*

Of course you are. They'd make sure it wouldn't be easy to find, he said tensely. *We're fifteen to thirty minutes out. Now that you've stopped moving, I shouldn't make any more wrong turns.*

Hopefully, you'll get here before anything bad happens. I wanted to hug him and never let him go. *She thinks the spell will take another couple of hours to wear off. I don't know why she thinks that, but I won't question it.*

Okay, I'll let you know when we're close. His voice broke. *Just promise me you'll do whatever is necessary to survive.*

I'd been in survival mode for as long as I could remember. Even if I didn't have him to live for, I wouldn't just roll over. I'd done that too often before getting away from Sarah, and I wouldn't keel over and give up now. *I promise.*

The door to the cabin creaked open, and we entered the house. The thick scent of dust settled deep into my lungs, giving me the urge to cough. I swallowed it down, wanting to appear as out of it as possible.

"Set her on the couch," Vera commanded as she walked deeper into the room. Her shoes echoed against the old wooden floors. "Make sure I can see her eyes."

Ollie walked over to a dusty fabric couch and dropped me on it. A cloud of dust puffed all around me.

"Where the hell are we?" He coughed and wiped his nose. "Looks like no one has been here in years."

"Try decades." Vera chuckled as she hovered over me, sneering at me with disgust. "At least, she's awake. I was worried the spell would knock her out. Now I don't have to wait to tell her why she's here."

That would be great information to start with. I blinked, hoping it wouldn't make her suspicious.

"You see, I came here looking for the dragon." Vera wrinkled her nose. The nerdy girl was gone. Her hair cascaded down her shoulders, and her glasses were missing. "I'd heard about the dragon and his friends and how they were coming back to Kortright."

Why would she be after Egan? He was a good person and never treated people poorly.

"I'm sure you're wondering why." She tapped her head. "You may not be able to speak or react, but I know how a woman in love reacts. It's really rather easy." She took a few steps away and placed her hands behind her back. "The dragons hurt everyone who gets in their way and need to be stopped."

"Maybe we should get out of here." Ollie rubbed his fingers along his pants. "I have a bad feeling about this."

"Shut it, bird," Vera snapped. "You're being paranoid like always."

Ollie's mouth clamped shut, and anger flared in his eyes.

"You see, I had a feeling the dragon would meet his mate, so we watched him. Any girl who got close to him, we killed, hoping he'd fly back to his thunder so we could locate their secret living place." Vera rolled her eyes. "I thought it was you, but the way you shut him down made me think I'd completely misread the situation. That was until I walked in on you Monday."

That was why she'd been so angry. She realized she'd made a mistake and the girl she'd been looking for was right under her nose. It had nothing to do with catching us in the act.

"I had to be smart after acting crazy, so I planned to get you from Haynes." She clenched her jaw, looking damn scary. "I should've known the dragon and his little squad wouldn't let you go off alone. He must have tracked Ollie there the week before when we killed that server girl."

Amber died because she'd been all over Egan. Now I felt bad for being so angry at her.

"You must be wondering why I'm telling you this." She gave me a sad smile. "I want you to understand that I'm righting a wrong from so many years ago. That this is very unfortunate—you actually were a decent roommate—but there is something so much bigger at play."

Her words and actions suggested sympathy, but the feeling was missing. There was a coldness to her that told me that she enjoyed doing all of these bad things. That she felt they were just and righteous.

It was the same gleam I'd seen in Sarah's eyes, and a realization settled heavily on my chest. That was the look that would be in Sarah's eyes right before she'd give me the strongest beating. So I already knew what would happen next.

CHAPTER TWENTY-TWO

V era would kill me soon. After the villains justify all of the reasons for their actions, they usually take action. So far, I was a means to an end, despite not being a horrible roommate.

A knife magically appeared in Vera's hand. "But most importantly, your death will not be in vain. Your death will mean something and will not go unfelt by your mate."

Mate.

Egan.

There was no way in hell I'd allow that to happen. I had too much to live for. Adrenaline coursed through me, and I welcomed it. There had to be a way out of this situation. My dragon surged inside.

"Isn't that what we all want?" The gleam in her eyes hardened. "To be loved and remembered?" She sneered as she raised the knife above her head and her gaze landed on my heart. "I'll make it quick, don't worry."

My dragon brushed against my brain, fueling my body. I didn't really know her yet, but I had a feeling we'd get more acquainted.

As Vera's hands slammed down, I kicked her in the stomach. She crashed against the wall.

Ollie froze and looked at Vera as she bounced off the wall. His mouth dropped, and his brows furrowed. "I thought you said—"

"I know what I said!" Vera screamed. Her breathing turned ragged as she glared at me. "How did you get the spell to wear off so quickly?"

Yeah, like I'd tell her that. I stood and lifted my chin. I'd fight them both. *How close are you?* With her witchy magic and Ollie transforming into a bird, I was at a disadvantage.

We're getting closer. Maybe ten minutes away. Egan's displeasure was clear. *Is something happening?*

Yeah, she tried to stab me. And I would kick the bitch's ass.

What? He growled, and the sound scared me. *Are you hurt?*

Okay, I should've maybe led into it more gently, but at least all his rage wasn't channeled toward me. *I'm fine, but get here as soon as you can.* I disconnected from him, needing to focus.

All of my years of martial arts had better pay off.

Vera sneered and threw the knife at me.

I ducked, and the knife passed over my head, the breeze hitting the top of my hair. I'd barely dodged it. I turned and found the knife lodged into the couch cushion, dust floating all around it.

"Get her!" Vera commanded Ollie.

Ollie moved immediately, stalking over to me. His gaze locked on my waist, making it obvious where he planned to attack.

He jumped, charging to sack me.

I turned to the side and kicked him in the chest.

Usually, the impact would have thrown me slightly off-balance, but it was like I'd kicked a soccer ball instead of a guy who weighed twenty pounds more than me. Further proof of how much I'd changed.

As he landed on the ground, Vera raced across the room toward me, aiming for my face. My arms flew up, blocking her assault. I grabbed her shoulders and tossed her to the ground.

"Ugh," she groaned as she crumpled to the floor.

Arms wrapped around my arms, restraining them. I leaned forward, causing Ollie to lose his balance and fall over my head. The hold on my arms lessened as he landed hard on his back.

I straightened and kicked him in the side, and he curled into a ball.

"You bitch," Vera spat, clambering to her feet. "I won't feel bad about this at all now."

Yeah, she hadn't before. Pleasure radiated off her. Now she'd be less rational and methodical, which would piss her off more. But I wasn't sure what a witch was capable of, so I didn't have a clue what to expect.

She ran over to the dirty plywood cabinets and pulled out a large steak knife.

What the hell was it with her and knives? I expected her to use magic, but she didn't seem inclined. Maybe she was trying to disarm me.

Instead of running at me, she walked slowly like she had a plan.

It was time for me to go on the offensive. I rushed at her, keeping focused on her. If I could break her leg, it would hinder her enough that I'd only need to focus on Ollie. Since she was holding a knife, I went with a kick.

Right before my foot connected with her knee, she

swung the knife downward, jamming it into my calf. It sank so deep it hit bone.

She stumbled against the counter as blinding pain seared up my leg. I fell to the ground, and a thick, metallic scent hit my nose. The knife stayed lodged in my leg.

Jade, you're hurt. Egan's voice was low and raw. *I'm shifting to get to you faster.*

I'd opened the bond up because of the sheer pain. I wanted to respond, but I couldn't.

I grabbed the handle and yanked before I could think too much about it. Blood poured from my wound, soaking my pant leg, and dripped into my shoe. Dammit, this would make fighting more difficult for several reasons—the pain, and my feet might slip in the blood.

My blood coated my hands, and I dropped the knife.

"Did you really think you could escape?" Vera laughed maniacally. "You may be turning into a dragon, but you're not there yet. And there are two of us against your one. Hell, you don't even know how to use your dragon yet. I bet the shifter hasn't taught you because he wants to be the one to protect you, but it's only given me the advantage."

If there was any truth to her words, I'd be addressing that with Egan—if I made it out of this alive. He needed to teach me, not shelter me.

Vera crouched over me with a cruel smirk and grabbed the knife. She wiped the blood off the blade on her black jeans without flinching. "All it takes is the right kind of wound."

I had no choice but to fight. If I didn't, I'd be dead. I slumped my shoulders despite my dragon roaring in my ears. She didn't want me to appear weak. She wanted us to die as warriors, but I had no intention of dying. "So this is how it ends? You kill me, and then what? If Egan goes back to his thunder, he won't make it easy for you to follow him."

"Please," she scoffed. "You really are stupid. He should've taught you everything before letting you join our world." She looked down her nose at me.

"You're going to get us killed," Ollie groaned as he stood, clutching his side. "You're wasting time. There's no telling when that spell wore off. That dragon could be here any second."

"Shut up!" she screamed, her face turning red as she stared at him. "I tell you what to do, not the other way around."

He flinched but shut up. His hands shook with either rage or fear. Maybe a combination of both.

"She needs to understand how she will be the fall of her mate and his family." She squatted next to me and smiled as she watched the blood pour from my wound.

A puddle of blood now surrounded my leg. I was bleeding a lot. If my blood loss continued at this rate, I'd get lightheaded and pass out. I had to kick her ass before then.

"Since you're his fated mate, I can use any part of you to locate him," she said with giddiness. "Your hair, your fingernail, your blood. Anything. I can find him through you because of that connection."

My blood turned to ice. This was a whole lot harder than I'd realized. Here I'd thought if I died, he would be safe, but he wouldn't. "Then why didn't you take something of mine back at the dorm?" There didn't have to be any senseless killing.

"Because he purposely doesn't go back to his thunder that often. We've watched, and he hasn't gone back since the beginning of spring semester." She glared. "Dragons are smart. They know how to stay hidden. I need to give him motivation to go back and rally his troops. That way, I can locate them, and Ollie can do the rest."

"What's so important about that journal?" If I kept her talking, I could buy Egan time to get here.

"Ah, that old thing?" Her eyes lit with pure rage. "That weaves my tale of how the love of my life did me wrong. And includes my plan for revenge. Just a few choice spells that will wreak havoc on the dragons."

Her grandmother was the one who'd gotten hurt, and that journal had fueled enough anger in her granddaughter to get revenge. Maybe their whole family was messed up. Anger could only get someone so far.

The threat against my thunder made my dragon roar inside me, and I punched Vera in the jaw. The crunch of bone sounded like a little victory in my ear.

Falling back on her ass, she clutched her jaw and dropped the knife. "Yuuu bshhh." Tears poured down her face, but her eyes were raw with pain.

Her mouth was crooked, evidence that I'd broken her jaw. Hopefully, that would even out the playing field.

Ollie rolled over and climbed to his feet. His eyes lacked the malice of Vera's, but he was gearing up to fight me again.

I rose to my feet, putting my weight on the uninjured leg. Fighting wouldn't come easy, but I couldn't lie down and die. I'd go out fighting.

He kicked my injured leg, and I fell back to the ground as nausea rolled through my stomach. I'd never been in so much pain in my life.

They circled me like I was the prey. Hell, I had to be honest.

I was their prey.

"Yu cud hv md this esy on yu," Vera growled. "Bt slw it isss."

"I don't like taking the easy way out. So, bring it on." If I appeared confident, maybe they'd hesitate.

Vera kicked me in the face. My head jerked back, and my neck popped.

I'm almost there. Egan linked; white-hot rage filled the bond. *Hang on, baby. Can you tell me what's going on and where you're injured?*

Hope sprung in my chest. He was close. I almost thought I wouldn't get out of this alive. *They're circling me. She stabbed me in the leg, all the way to the bone.*

All I had to do was make her put off killing me a little longer.

I rubbed my neck, trying to massage the pain away. "You'll never take them down. Egan will find you and kill you."

"Lts hooop sssooo." She leaned down and pressed the knife against my neck. A trickle of blood dripped down my neck and onto my white shirt.

That was all I needed—more blood loss.

A roar shook the cabin as the loud flapping of wings sounded outside.

"Holy shit!" Ollie yelled. "The dragon is here."

She turned her head to the side, shifting her arm. A bracelet I'd never noticed before appeared from underneath her long shirt sleeve. The old sterling silver band had seen better days, but the stone was the most interesting part. The stone was clear, reminding me of a quartz, but the black flecks inside looked like ash. A thick, sturdy clasp at its base prevented it from coming off easily.

My dragon caressed my brain, and I understood her for once. She was telling me that only something important would be locked up that tight.

I took a deep breath to calm my nerves as she dug the knife in deeper.

Ollie's voice grew high as he said, "We have to end this now and run."

"No, he wn't hut us as lnng ss we uus hr ss a shieeeld." Her eyes flicked to the door, which was all I needed. I sat up, snatched the hand that held the knife, and removed the weapon with my free one.

Vera jerked back, trying to pull from my grasp. My fingers curled around the bracelet, and I yanked it hard. The clasp broke.

"Nooo," she gasped, and her nails sank into my arm, tearing into my flesh. She clawed at me desperately, trying to get the bracelet back.

I hit her in the head with the butt of the knife, and she dropped.

Now my attention was on Ollie, who was staring at the door, not paying attention to his surroundings. I stood, clutching the knife and bracelet securely.

I had to put him down. I attempted to rush him, but my feet tripped over each other as my peripheral vision darkened and blurred. The blood loss was finally catching up to me. Ollie grabbed the wrist of my hand holding the knife and pressed his thumb against mine. The weapon fell to the floor. He spun me around so my back was against his stomach, and he placed his knife against my throat.

His breathing became labored, and something large slammed against the outside of the cabin. After another large ram, the walls crumbled as a dragon stepped through the debris.

Egan was here.

My eyes took in his gigantic form. He was as large as the cabin and had dark olive-green scales. His golden eyes were as bright as the sun as they zeroed in on Ollie and the knife at my neck.

He threw his head back and roared; flames spilled from his mouth.

No one had to be a dragon to understand the message: *Let her go now.*

"I can't." Ollie's hand shook as he dug the knife deeper into my neck.

Feeling blissfully numb, I sagged against Ollie's chest. My body grew heavy, and it was too hard to keep myself upright. It took every ounce of strength I had to keep my eyes open. *I don't know how much longer I can last.*

The dragon took several menacing steps toward us and opened his mouth, revealing his sharp, jagged teeth. *I'm getting you out of here.* He hissed, blowing hot smoke in our direction.

"Ddd it!" Vera screamed. "Kll hr nw!" Her voice was wild and crazed as she ran behind us.

Ollie dug the knife in deeper. This was the end.

Tears burned my eyes, and the most important words I'd ever said ran through my head. *I love you.*

ABOUT THE AUTHOR

Jen L. Grey is a *USA Today* Bestselling Author who writes Paranormal Romance, Urban Fantasy, and Fantasy genres.

Jen lives in Tennessee with her husband, two daughters, and two miniature Australian Shepherd. Before she began writing, she was an avid reader and enjoyed being involved in the indie community. Her love for books eventually led her to writing. For more information, please visit her website and sign up for her newsletter.

Check out my future projects and book signing events at my website.
www.jenlgrey.com

ALSO BY JEN L. GREY

Shadow City: Silver Wolf Trilogy

Broken Mate

Rising Darkness

Silver Moon

Shadow City: Royal Vampire Trilogy

Cursed Mate

Shadow Bitten

Demon Blood

Shadow City: Royal Vampire Trilogy

Ruined Mate

Shattered Curse

Fated Souls

The Hidden King Trilogy

Dragon Mate

Dragon Heir

Dragon Queen

The Wolf Born Trilogy

Hidden Mate

Blood Secrets

Awakened Magic

The Marked Wolf Trilogy

Moon Kissed

Chosen Wolf

Broken Curse

Wolf Moon Academy Trilogy

Shadow Mate

Blood Legacy

Rising Fate

The Royal Heir Trilogy

Wolves' Queen

Wolf Unleashed

Wolf's Claim

Bloodshed Academy Trilogy

Year One

Year Two

Year Three

The Half-Breed Prison Duology (Same World As Bloodshed Academy)

Hunted

Cursed

The Artifact Reaper Series

Reaper: The Beginning

Reaper of Earth

Reaper of Wings

Reaper of Flames

Reaper of Water

Stones of Amaria (Shared World)

Kingdom of Storms

Kingdom of Shadows

Kingdom of Ruins

Kingdom of Fire

The Pearson Prophecy

Dawning Ascent

Enlightened Ascent

Reigning Ascent

Stand Alones

Death's Angel

Rising Alpha

Printed in Great Britain
by Amazon